Gore in the *Garden*

A Collection Of Cozies

Shelley Dawn Siddall

Gore in the *Garden*

A Collection of Cozies

Shelley Dawn Siddall

Shelley Dawn Siddall

Copyright

The right of Shelley Dawn Siddall to be identified as the Author of the work has been asserted by her in accordance with the Copyright, Designs and Patents Act 1988.

All rights reserved.

The book is copyright material and must not be copied, reproduced, transferred, distributed, leased, licensed, or publicly performed or used in any way except as specifically permitted in writing by the publisher, as allowed under the terms and conditions under which it was purchased or as strictly permitted by applicable copyright law. Any unauthorized distribution or use of this text may be a direct infringement of the author's and publisher's rights and those responsible may be liable in law accordingly.

Gore in the Garden, A Collection of Cozies, is a work of fiction. Names, characters, businesses, organizations, places, events, and incidents are either the product of the author's imagination or are used fictiously. Any resemblance to actual persons, living or dead, events or locales is entirely coincidental.

Copyright © 2021 Shelley Dawn Siddall
All rights reserved.
ISBN 9798749981919
Cover Design by www.mariahsinclair.com

Dedication

To my dear Sister Tracy Zawitkoski, who laughed in all the right places and lit a fire under my butt to keep writing, instead of watching TV and eating frozen cappuccino yogurt.
And I really like frozen cappuccino yogurt so clearly, she is a force to be reckoned with.
And admired.

Shelley Dawn Siddall

Table of Contents

Gore in the *Garden* ....

Copyright iv

Dedication v

Scarecrows Don't Bleed 1

Don't Be Koi With Me! 26

How To Refuse An Offer 46

Canoodling in the Carnations 63

Reap What You Sow? 78

Mr. Pitre, Pickled And Potted In The Garden 97

The Garden Rake or Lettuce Alone! 110

How to Water Your Garden by Kicking the Bucket 119

A Garden Party for Death 144

Dropping Beets 157

Thyme to Die 175

Don't Get Up On The Wrong Side Of The Bed! 194

What Happens When The Cabbage Leaves? 207

About the Author 220

Scarecrows Don't Bleed

Gracie Noseworthy liked cats better than dogs. Cats knew who they were and let you know immediately if you were out of line. Cats could actually plot revenge for days, attack you for the slightest infraction, (say a minute delay in serving them a meal), but surprised you with a random cuddle.

Dogs, on the other hand, could spend hours pushing a rock with their nose and be entirely happy the whole time. Gracie found their constant state of bliss annoying.

She lived in a small town with quaint homes and not so quaint people who regularly said to folks in the big cities they visited, 'I come from a town so small you know everybody's name and even the names of their dogs!' But when asked the name of their neighbor, or even to just describe what their neighbor looked like, most residents then mumbled something about not really knowing them.

Oh, they might have taken them to court over property lines or other trivial matters, but even then, they didn't know them. They may, however, know the name of the dog.

The town was, quite frankly, full of bad neighbors with bad habits.

Shelley Dawn Siddall

Gracie thrived on the disputes of her neighbors because she liked a little drama in her life. She liked her unpredictable cats, Zoey, and Frank, and she liked unpredictable people. That's why, after she retired from retail, Gracie put an ad in the Huckleberry News that read as follows:

"Did you do something bad, but can't quite remember? Did your neighbor do something bad, and you want to get the goods on them? Contact Gracie Noseworthy Investigations at 555-2368. I sniff out trouble!"

So when the woman at the other end of the phone line said, "I know something bad about my neighbor; at least, I think I do," Gracie felt a tingle of excitement and immediately invited her over for tea and a chat.

"Well, I don't know if I should," the woman said plaintively, "I don't want to get anybody in trouble."

"But you have phoned me," Gracie noted. "You must be fairly certain you saw something untoward. My standard fee is one hundred dollars to open a file, paid up front in cash or bank draft. For this sum, I will find out what happened and report back to you. Expenses will be extra. You of course will have access to unlimited pots of tea at my home during the interview process."

"I suppose I could come by this afternoon."

Gracie had to be firm. "I have an opening in my schedule right now until five pm. I am otherwise engaged the rest of the evening."

"Oh. Well then. I'll pop by the bank and come straight over."

"I'll need your name please, so I can start your file," Gracie said, pencil poised over her desk calendar.

"Barbara Shire, but my friends call me Barb."

Gracie smiled into the phone. "See you soon Barb. I'll be happy to take on your case."

Gore in the *Garden*

When the new client arrived, she reminded Gracie of a pug. Slightly googly eyed and snuffling. And a bit gassy.

They were sitting at Gracie's large kitchen table that her late husband, Stan, had built. Both leaves were in and as such the table was a good four feet wide by eight feet, eight inches long. Wide enough to place soup tureens, platters of cold cuts and freshly baked bread in between twelve guests. Gracie loved hosting lunches. It gave her ample opportunity to sniff out fractious undercurrents and gossip that always came in handy.

She poured out some rich vanilla rooibos and asked Barb to tell her what happened.

"It's just that I don't want to get anybody in trouble," Barb started.

Gracie had already put the cash in her lockbox, so she felt it necessary to encourage Barb again to start talking. But Gracie thought, if she keeps prevaricating, I'll ask her to leave and refund her money. Maybe.

"My neighbor killed somebody and dumped the body in the field across from me. I know because he had it in a wheelbarrow and wheeled it right in front of me!"

"When did this happen?"

"The night before last. I was out for an evening stroll…"

Here Gracie raised her eyebrows. It was still quite chilly in the evening and the snuffling pudgy woman in front of her did not look the least bit athletic.

"Probably how you got your cold," Gracie said.

Barb looked startled. "Yes!" she said enthusiastically, "I was out for an evening stroll Tuesday and I got a cold. Don't get me wrong, I always get along with people, but my neighbor is another kettle of fish. Do you know, he went and got married? In February?"

Gracie clapped her hands. "I saw the photo spread in the newspaper! That was the Frederickson-Ellis wedding, wasn't it? The bride was stunning in a daring baby blue gown!"

"She was an icicle," Barb said smugly. "I happened to be walking by and saw them posing in the park for photos. She was shivering and actually turning blue. I thought she was going to freeze to death right there. Would have served her right."

Her Hostess wrote in large letters on a piece of foolscap 'neighbor had body in wheelbarrow'. Gracie had the paper angled so her client could easily read the notes. It was a ploy she used to make her clients think that *their focus* was Gracie's focus.

Gracie was actually making mental notes that ran like this, 'No ring on left hand, jilted ex-lover? Is there even a body? Has that woman been eating nothing but cabbage for three days straight? Land sakes, the smell!'

"What time was it that you were out for your stroll?"

"What stroll?" Barb asked.

Gracie smiled encouragingly and pointed to the pad of paper. "Your stroll on Tuesday evening? When the body in the wheelbarrow was wheeled right by you?"

Her client dabbed at her nose with a frilly hanky. "Oh yes, of course, silly me, the cold medicine must be mixing me up. It was just after supper, perhaps around six, and I thought I would go to the end of my drive and see if the crocuses were peeking through yet. I was moving the dead leaves from under the maple, I have a Crimson King maple in the front of my property, when I saw Barry, I mean, Mr. Frederickson pushing a wheelbarrow."

"And then what happened?"

"Well naturally I said good evening."

Gracie could barely restrain a sigh. Let's liven things up a bit, she decided.

"The new Mrs. Frederickson was walking with him?" she asked.

Gore in the *Garden*

"Are you kidding? And risk breaking one of her five-inch heels? No Anita wasn't with Barry. It was just him."

"And his wheelbarrow," Gracie added.

"Right. He thinks he's the world's greatest gardener, but when he cut my maple last year, I could have throttled him! I mean, when we had that big windstorm in November, my poor tree had huge branches that came crashing down. Barry offered to trim it up for me and he butchered the thing. So when I saw him, I may have said a few choice words to him."

"What did the wheelbarrow look like?" Gracie asked as she eyed the liquor cabinet behind her loquacious but unforthcoming client.

"It was orange, with red splotches all over it. Oh yes, one handle was gone. The wood around the metal I mean, it was broken off."

"And what did the body look like?"

Barb pondered while she spent some time trying to create a sneeze by looking at Gracie's dining room chandelier.

"It looked dead," she said finally.

"Was it a man or a woman?" Gracie asked while hoping she had, in fact, filled the ice cube tray the previous night. Her thoughts continued to turn to a rum and coke over ice.

"It was a man, I think. He had on a checkered shirt, like scarecrows wear and old dungarees and a straw hat over his face. Barry did, in fact, say it was a scarecrow he was moving to another part of his land. But here's the funny thing, Barry was headed to the empty field across the road from both our places."

"I take it he doesn't own that particular field?"

"No, it's been for vacant for years." She sniffed loudly. "Apparently the ownership of the land is in dispute."

Gracie poured Barb another cup of tea. "So Barry was transporting a dead body. Who do you think he killed?

Barb's face darkened. She crossed her arms and slid her chair back from the table.

"Oh I wouldn't have any idea! Why would I know?" she retorted.

The two women went on to discuss Barry and his wife's work schedules, that Barb just happened to know, and concluded their meeting shortly before the imposed deadline.

Gracie grimaced as Barb picked up the hanky off the oak table, but quickly smiled as she waved her client goodbye. As soon as Barb's little Toyota rounded the bend in Gracie's driveway, Gracie was on the phone.

"Change in plans Ted, we're going to meet at my place and drink rum until the memory of my latest client is gone."

"On my way," he said.

***

One hour and several drinks later Gracie and her assistant Ted Bailey were summing up the latest case. He had extra information that he readily shared.

"We were called out for a report of a suspected stalker in early March, but after a thorough search of the grounds we didn't even find a fresh footprint," Ted commented. He said wryly, "I think the frozen layer of snow may have been an impediment. Anita was not pleased. She called us slackers and wanted us to arrest somebody immediately!"

Ted had an expressive set of bushy gray eyebrows; was a Detective Sergeant in the local police force and one of Gracie's oldest and dearest friends. He had joined the force at the same time as Stan Noseworthy when both men were single. Ted married his childhood sweetheart, Laura-Beth, shortly afterwards, Gracie and Stan were happily married.

In a weird twist of fate, Ted and Gracie lost their mates to cancer about one year apart from each other. Many of their friends and acquaintances felt that Ted and Gracie should be married by now as they spent considerable time together, however the investigative team had a completely different arrangement that worked for them.

"The peeping Tom probably was Barb. She sure seems to do a lot of walking at key moments." Gracie counted on her fingers. "One, she just happened to be walking by the wedding, two, she happened to be walking by when Barry was overtly wheeling a dead body, and three, she really doesn't like Anita."

Ted nodded and asked, "I'll check and see if anyone has been reported missing. From everything you've told me, Barb and Barry were quite chummy, or at least she thought they were. I mean, a man prunes your tree, that's got to mean something!" He waggled his eyebrows at his friend/part-time boss.

Gracie smiled. "I imagine the marriage to Anita Ellis must have come as a bit of a shock. Ted, there was something else," Gracie said eyeing her watch. "Barb's body language was wrong. She got defensive when I asked about who the dead person could be. She pushed herself away from the table as though to distance herself from the whole event."

Ted too, was looking at his watch. "Well Gracie my dear, I'm glad we didn't meet for supper as planned. This has been fun, but right now, do you know what's on the agenda?"

"Bowling!" Gracie said happily.

Ted drained his drink and leapt to his feet. "The Huckleberry Blue Balls are ready to roll!"

Despite herself Gracie snickered. There had been much discussion on the police force about the name of their bowling team. Everybody had been loudly yelling their favorite name while at the same time condemning Ted's suggestion.

Unfortunately, Ted was the only one sober enough to think of registering the name. Although not a constable, Gracie was now an honorary member of the Huckleberry Blue Balls. However, when asked what team she was on, she always said 'Huckleberry Blue' then paused before adding 'Balls'.

"We have to change that name!" Gracie said as they walked out the door.

She returned to give Zoey and Frank some instructions.

"Now look folks," she said sternly, "You are both grown cats. I do not, repeat, do not want to find that you had a party while I was gone. I've marked the levels in the liquor bottles and locked up all the toilet paper. Be good."

The two cats waited until Gracie had left the house and then ran to the en-suite. The toilet paper roll had not, in fact, been locked up.

***

"I think she should be locked up! I mean, her garden is a blight on the neighborhood!"

Gracie and Ted looked at one another as they were tying up their rented shoes, then over at the speaker.

"I haven't said anything to her before now, you know it wouldn't be kind so soon after her husband left her, but I do intend to bring the matter to the Garden Club after a decent interval." Trudy-Faye Gervais was pontificating to her team, the Holy Rollers, one lane over.

As Ted laid out the score sheets and the pencils, he asked Gracie, "Have you ever found the volume control on Trudy-Faye?"

"Nope and I'm not looking for it," Gracie said as she tied up her long silver hair in a ponytail.

"Chicken."

Gore in the *Garden*

"In other, more pressing matters, my dear Theodore, where are your brothers and your sister in blue? It's nearly seven."

"I gave Mark an extra assignment. Pauline and Dave should be here any minute now."

At that moment, the three team members entered the Splitsville Lanes. While the married couple went to rent shoes, Mark walked over to Ted with several sheets of paper in his hand.

"Got that information you asked for. Looks like Barb Shire has had a few run-ins with her neighbors."

"Do tell!" said Gracie.

"She's due in court tomorrow for mediation with Andrew Walters, the neighbor to the right of her from the street view, while the neighbor to the left of her is in the process of obtaining a restraining order." Mark dutifully reported to his boss but showed the documents to Gracie.

Ted reached over and took the documents.

"Could we at least pretend that I have some degree of confidentiality regarding police matters?" he asked Gracie.

She smiled. "So it was Anita Frederickson who filed the restraining order, but what was the other neighbor upset about?"

"Dang, you read fast," Mark said. He went to rent shoes as Ted perused the reports.

"Looks like he applied for a restraining order as well," Ted said, "and was granted one. Barb Shire continually harassed him for years about a piece of property that she said he promised her, get this, 'as a wedding gift'."

"What? Does that woman think everybody is in love with her?"

Ted started chuckling as he read further. "This is cute. Andrew Walters wrote in his application, 'I have no interest, nor have I ever had any interest in becoming betrothed to that woman. Her name should be Barbed Wire instead of Barb Shire as she is constantly poking around my house."

Ted's laughter abruptly stopped as he continued, "When she doesn't get invited in, she says cutting remarks and has threatened to shoot me several times. I didn't take her seriously at first, but she brought her twelve gauge over in February and waved it around."

Gracie frowned as well. "You'd think the recoil of a twelve gauge would knock old Barbed Wire off her feet. But more importantly, she brought a gun to his home. And here I was thinking of her as a harmless, if somewhat gassy, little pug."

Pauline, Dave, and Mark had already taken their turns. Ted rolled a spare and Gracie ended up with a bedpost split. She glared at the seven and ten pins.

"They should really change the name of this bowling alley," she declared.

"Bedposts! She planted bedposts!" Trudy-Faye shouted to her team after watching Gracie gutter the ball while attempting to pick up a spare.

Gracie walked over. "What in the world are you talking about?"

Trudy-Faye was red in the face from the exertion of throwing three strikes in a row while at the same time, giving a running commentary on her strategy. Now that her audience had increased; so did her color.

"Let's sit you down and give you some water," Gracie added.

"You know Julia Smith? The one whose husband took off with the young woman from the tanning salon?"

Gracie didn't know her but nodded anyway.

"Well, she went to the dump and dragged all manner of trash home including old metal headboards and footboards. She put them in her garden and planted mounds of marigolds in between."

"Oh! So she really does have garden beds. How cute!" Gracie said enthusiastically, but then looked at Trudy-Faye's face.

"But not a good look really," she added.

Gore in the *Garden*

After the President of the Garden Club's face returned to normal, Gracie returned to the game. She was still a bit woozy from her liquid supper but was determined to make her 148 average. She missed by two points.

"Instead of drowning my sorrows, you know what would make me feel better?" she asked Ted.

"Food?"

"Almost. Let's go take a look at that land across from Barbed Wire's place."

***

The flashlight illuminated an orange wheelbarrow with red splotches and missing one wooden handle.

"The body is missing though," Gracie said.

"If there ever was a body. Let's come back early in the morning and look around. I'm not on shift until nine."

"I'm not even out of bed until nine!" Gracie suddenly stepped forward and ran her finger over the edge of the wheelbarrow. She sniffed her finger.

"This is blood, Ted. I'm fairly certain scarecrows don't bleed."

"Maybe the scarecrow walked home. It is odd though, that Miss Shire got this much of the information correct. I mean, this is a pretty distinctive wheelbarrow. It will be easy to trace the owner and if they're complicit in a murder, why bother to get rid of the body?" Ted mused. "Well, we'll check it out in the morning."

"Do you suppose scarecrows' houses are made of straw?" Gracie asked as she continued to search around the wheelbarrow. She added, "Mind you, that would be kind of gross because when you think about it. Scarecrows are stuffed with straw so essentially they would be building a house out of their innards."

Ted sighed. "How your mind works continually surprises me."

Shelley Dawn Siddall

***

As soon as Gracie unlocked her front door, two things happened. She let out a horrendous sneeze and her cell phone rang.

"Well?"

Gracie mopped up her face and answered, "I'm okay thanks. Who is this?"

"It's Barb Shire. What did you find out?"

"Quite a number of things actually. Things like restraining orders…" Gracie said as she started turning on several lights. There was a suspicious fluffiness to the air. Zoey and Frank ran up to greet her and began curling around her ankles.

"What did you do?" she demanded of her cats.

There was a gasp on the other end of the line.

"That Anita is such a hag. Before she showed up, it was Barb and Barry, Barry, and Barb. Don't those names sound just perfect together?"

Gracie walked into her bedroom and spied a pile of unrolled toilet paper on the floor of the en-suite. She looked down at her cats, who were purring mightily.

"Making a nest, were you?" she asked the cats.

"Of course I was!" Barb said haughtily. "After all, Barry spent hours pruning my maple and hauling all the debris away. A man doesn't do that for free unless he's trying to impress somebody!"

"You have a point there," Gracie said. Not a correct point, but a point nonetheless she thought.

"Did you find the wheelbarrow?"

"Yes we did. Exactly where you said it would be. We did not however, find a body inside of it."

"Is that a problem?"

Gore in the *Garden*

Gracie bent down to pat her cats. As usual, she was more amused by their antics than angry. In dulcet tones she said to them, "I'm not angry at what you did; we all make mistakes don't we? Going forward, let's not do this again shall we?"

Her caller was over the moon with happiness.

"I knew another woman would see it my way! Best one hundred dollars I've ever spent! Thanks for agreeing with me." Barbed Wire hung up.

Gracie didn't know what she was agreeing to, and why Barb felt her money was well spent but Gracie was more convinced than ever that there was a dead body somewhere! In the meantime, a nightcap and a cuddle with the kitties was on the agenda.

***

Barb Shire put down her phone and walked to her linen closet. Her plan had come off without a hitch, so she deserved a celebration.

She was going to play dress-up.

Barb opened up her step stool, climbed up and reached for the very special white box on the highest shelf. Her short portly frame was stretched to its limit as she carefully inched the box closer. There! She had the edge of it, but an inopportune rumbling in her stomach began.

She tooted.

Out of habit, she said, "Oh excuse me," as her hands flew to cover her bottom. As she was falling she fleetingly wondered why she had to be so damn polite when no one was around.

The box landed on top of her as she slid to a sitting position. Her arm had been scraped up and was bleeding slightly. What Barb really wanted to do she couldn't. She didn't dare risk soiling the white bridal gown lovingly wrapped in acid free tissue paper and preserved in the very pretty white box.

She sighed and walked to her living room where a robust Aloe Vera plant was growing and cut a piece from it with the shears she always kept handy to protect herself at a moment's notice.

You never knew who might be snooping around! A girl had to defend herself after all. It was a good thing one of her foster families had trained her how to shoot a shotgun. Between the shears and the shotgun, she was ready to run off any intruders.

Sadly, they never intruded.

Well, Barry would be knocking at her door pretty soon when he learned what she had done for him. As she applied the aloe to her scrape, Barb thought of the effort she had expended two nights ago to get rid of that body for Barry.

She had been out walking on her property but within visual range of Barry's place, well, with the use of her binoculars, when she saw the ugly orange pushcart outside Barry's front door. There was a body in it.

"He's done it; he's killed the hag!" she said aloud.

She climbed the fence that ran along the property line and crept up to the house. The motion detector flooded the yard with light, so she quickly grabbed a stick and knocked it down. Unfortunately, the light had revealed that the corpse was male. Anita was probably still alive in the house, dang the luck.

On the positive side, even though both cars were in the garage, no one came to the door.

Probably playing dominoes together Barb thought sourly. She couldn't imagine that twig thin Anita could have the strength to kill anyone, so it must have been Barry. She shone the flashlight on the body as she lifted up the straw hat. Barb wasn't a squeamish woman, but she really wished she hadn't lifted the hat. Most of the damage was there.

Gore in the *Garden*

She didn't recognize the man, but he did look vaguely familiar. What to do? First, she had to protect her Barry. She had failed him in February when she couldn't stop that hag from getting her hooks in him, but by golly, she was going to help him now! Barb rolled the garish wheelbarrow to the fence and attempted to lift the body. No dice. She tried to lift a leg but that only shifted the body enough to cause an arm to flop down.

"Now I know why it's called dead weight," she whispered as the body did not cooperate. Finally she hit upon an idea. She dumped the body out by tipping the wheelbarrow on its side. From there she rolled the body under the fence to her property. She gave it one great push and rolled it down the gentle slope to her garden pond.

It didn't take much to push the corpse the final few inches into the pond. It sunk, but Barb was savvy enough to know that in a week or so, it would reappear. Well, she'd come up with a plan. For now, she retrieved the bloody straw hat, weighed it down with some of her smaller lawn ornaments and dumped it in the pond.

Then she headed back to Barry's.

This time, she decided not to climb over the fence. Barb felt like an action hero now and threw herself to the ground. In her mind, she was going to roll under the fence and immediately hop up with lightning speed for the next phase of her plan.

She landed with a solid thump in the dirt and then struggled to squeeze under the fence. Even though gravity was doing most of the work as she was pushing the empty wheelbarrow down the driveway, Barb was wheezing like a freight train.

It was the most physical work she had done in years. When she returned home that night she had a hot bath and reviewed her plan. If someone finds the wheelbarrow, they'll easily trace it back to Barry. He'll become unhinged because he'll think the body was discovered as well. But glory days! The body is in my pond! Won't he be grateful when I tell him I moved it! Then, speaking of moving, he'll move out the skinny chick and move me in!

Now it was Thursday night, and things were really clipping along at a good speed. New diet going well? Check. Figure out how to get someone to discover the wheelbarrow? Check.

Barb put a bandage on her arm. Actually, she thought, that Noseworthy broad wasn't such a bad sort for a slim gal. She wasn't skinny like Anita, and even though Gracie had somehow figured out that Barb had taken the body, she didn't blame her.

Barb gently opened the box and carefully lifted up the wedding gown over her head. It fit snugly. As usual, it filled Barb with such a sense of hope that her fantasies would soon become realities, that she started to have a conversation with her new husband.

"You know Barry, I should be sad that someone died, but it paved the way for us to be together finally. And really, I should be scared that you killed someone, but I'm sure you had a good reason darling. Let's dance."

The little chubby woman, grinned and snuffled as she danced in front of her full-length mirror. She started to close her eyes in ecstasy when she quickly opened them wide.

"It was Andrew Walters! That's who it was!"

***

Gracie had driven her own car the next morning to rendezvous with Ted at the unholy hour of seven o'clock. Ted hadn't arrived yet but fortunately, Gracie had a large travel mug full of strong coffee so she turned on the radio and settled in. In two minutes, she got bored.

"You snooze, you lose," she said as she got out of her car. She grabbed a stick and started poking around the long grass determined to find a clue before Ted showed up.

Gore in the *Garden*

After ten minutes, she failed to find a clue or a body for that matter.

"Now if I were a murderer, transporting a body in the dark, what would I not see, but a sharp investigator like Gracie Noseworthy would see in the day?"

She turned as she heard a car approaching, but it just drove by. Where was Ted? Gracie looked over at Barb Shire's house. It was surprisingly a pleasant looking brick home, with an abundance of tidy gardens. At the bottom of the yard, close to the road, was a beautiful little pond, surrounded by ornamental grasses and lilies.

The house to the right of Barb's was tidy as well but had a sad appearance.

"Sad? I must be down a quart." Gracie took another large gulp of coffee and continued to stare at the house.

Now why do I think it looks sad? she thought. The color was a dark gray, but compared to Barb's gorgeous red brick, it looked faded.

There were no flowers. Anywhere. While the house to the right of Barb's had the same expanse of yard, there were no pots, no hanging baskets, nothing except three metal butterflies.

She shook her head and gave a cursory glance inside the wheelbarrow. Her mind started to drift towards Trudy-Faye's' complaint about the woman who planted bedposts and marigolds.

Gracie knew she had a bit of a unique way of looking at some things, but she also knew that her subconscious worked overtime to notify her when it captured a clue. She therefore pursued this latest tangent. There were no marigolds in the wheelbarrow, but, upon closer inspection, there were two tiny spots of yellow. She leaned forward to investigate when she heard Ted yell.

"Don't touch anything!"

Startled, Gracie backed away but advised, "There's something in here you should look at. It might be important."

"Didn't mean to give you a fright, Gracie, but since we last spoke there have been some new developments."

Gracie continued to point to the yellow spots with her stick but looked at Ted and raised her eyebrows.

"The Dispatcher received two calls last night. One she thought was a prank call, but she sent an officer out to investigate. The other was a wellness check. Turns out that Barb's one neighbor was reported missing by his daughter while at the same time, Barb's other neighbor phoned in a murder."

"Say what?"

Ted pointed to Andrew Walter's sad gray home.

"Apparently his daughter calls him every night at nine thirty and he didn't answer so she waited and then called him again after an hour. He still didn't answer so a car was sent for a wellness check. About thirty minutes later, a male called in confessing to murder."

Gracie turned her head slightly, gave the mysterious yellow spots a quick poke with her stick and asked what the man said when he confessed.

"Relinquish the stick, madam, or I won't tell you."

Ted took the meekly offered stick and threw it behind him.

"The crime scene guys will be here shortly; I'll have to explain why your fingerprint will be in the blood; I don't need to have to further explain why you destroyed evidence."

Gracie started to say something, but Ted frowned. She sighed deeply and motioned for him to continue.

"It was Barry Frederickson who phoned in around midnight. To quote, "Heah I see you guys at the house one over. Do you think you could come and see me? I've had the strangest dream for the past three nights. I think I killed somebody."

"Well that actually fits with what Barbed Wire told me," Gracie said as she glanced at Barb's house. "But why did he think he was dreaming?"

Gore in the *Garden*

"I got a call around twelve thirty this morning; the officer figured I should be there for the interview. When we arrived at the Frederickson home, Barry was snoring loudly on the couch and Anita was saying Barry had been hallucinating about seeing a body in a wheelbarrow on Tuesday night. He had been anxious ever since, so she was slipping him some of her Ativan."

Gracie watched as Barb rolled a huge concrete planter into her pond.

"Well that's unusual," she said as she watched her client go up the hill and roll another planter down to the pond.

"Yes," Ted said, oblivious to the events going on behind him. "What made it more unusual is how much Anita tried to downplay Barry's confession. My spidy sense was tingling as soon as we drove up to the home. There was a busted motion detector light above the door, but more interesting was…" Ted stopped his tale and looked at Gracie.

"Do you have any of that coffee left?" he pleaded, "I've been up pretty much all night."

"You can drink it all if you keep talking."

Ted swallowed a large gulp and continued with the story, "There was a large blast mark on the siding and on the concrete steps, as though someone was using a power washer for the first time. Interestingly, there happened to be a power washer sitting right beside the door. So I'm talking to Anita, and she's acting antsy. So I decide to pull an old Columbo trick. I pretend we're going to leave, then I turn and scratch my head and ask her "Was it hard to use the power washer to wash the blood off?"

"And what did she say?"

"That's the funny part. The Columbo trick worked. She says, "Of course it was, it was the first time I used the power washer thingy and I had to get the blood off before Barry came home. I broke my nails trying to stuff old Andrew in the wheelbarrow after

I bashed him on the head, but I broke even more using the power washer."

By this time, Gracie's mouth was hanging open. "Did she even realize what she was saying?"

"No. She just kept going. Her plan was to kill Andrew and blame Barb, but because she broke her nails she decided to move the body over to Barb's later on."

Gracie rocked back and forth on her heels as she looked at her own sculpted nails.

"Prompt attention to any breakage is so important in proper care of one's nails," she intoned. Then she slapped her thigh and said with amazement, "I can't believe it! She commits a murder then goes and files her nails! How cold hearted is that? So, where was the body and was it really the neighbor Andrew?"

Ted gulped some more coffee. "We may have a situation there," he said. "At this time, we have no body. Or as Anita explained to us last night, no make it this morning, that she met Barry when he came home from a late shift and hustled him past the body. After she had filed her nails, she went out to take the body over to Barb's, but it was gone. So, despite arresting her for murder, we have to come up with some evidence in order to make the charge stick."

Gracie was distracted. She tapped one of her lovely high cheekbones and said slowly, "Well look at that. She did it again."

Ted was confused. "Who did what again?"

Gracie focus snapped into place.

"Two questions Ted. One, what color nail polish was Anita wearing and two, would you like to know where Andrew's body is?"

The Detective let out his breath slowly and shrugged.

"Not really, it's been a long night. Perhaps I'll just go home for a shower and a nap, except I can't do that because you know."

"You have a murderer to convict?" Gracie asked.

"No," Ted said slowly, "It's just that I hate to go to bed with bad breath."

Gracie smiled and nodded. "I see. What you're saying is you left your toothbrush at my house again. Well you know Zoey and Frank have probably used it by now."

Ted smiled back. "Yellow. Her nail polish was yellow and yes I would like to know where the body is."

His friend didn't say anything but walked by him and picked up the stick he had discarded. She pointed at the wheelbarrow.

"At least two broken fingernails of the painted yellow variety are stuck in a pool of dried blood yonder." Gracie then pointed forcefully at Barb's house. "And speaking of pools, I believe Miss Barbara Shire has been desperately trying to weigh something down. Since you have arrived, she has rolled three huge planters into her pond. I suspect a dead body may be underneath them all."

***

"He hasn't shown up," the clerk said to Barb later that morning at the courthouse.

It was 10:30. He was thirty minutes late.

Barb shrugged and tried to appear indifferent, but she felt a smile creeping around the edges of her mouth. She was pretty sure that her neighbor would never show up. Especially since she rolled some heavy concrete planters in the pond early this morning a couple of hours before she left.

The Noseworthy chick and the cop were already investigating the wheelbarrow. After Barb showered and ate breakfast, she peeked out the window, and glory be, a whole passel of cops had shown up and were across the road. They eventually loaded the wheelbarrow in a small truck and drove away. They'd never find the body though. Of that she was certain.

She started giggling at the thought.

"Now what happens?" she asked the clerk, knowing the answer.

The clerk walked into the middle of the waiting room and called again, "In the matter of Walters mediation with Shire, are the parties present?" She sighed and added, "Is there a Mr. Walters, a Mr. Andrew Walters present?"

Barb covered her smile with a frilly hanky and coughed.

"As Mr. Walters has failed to appear, you are free to leave. He will have to re-apply for mediation. Looks like this is your lucky day."

You don't know the half of it, Barb thought as she raced out of the courthouse and ran headlong into Barry.

"Barb! What are you doing here?" he asked.

"As if you don't know, you sly dog you," Barb said with a smirk on her face.

Barry frowned and shook his head. "Whatever Barb, I have to go." He started up the stairs then turned back and hollered, "Anita got arrested this morning! For murder!"

Every cell in Barb Shire's body was immediately charged with electricity as she repeated each word.

"Anita got arrested this morning? For murder? This day just keeps getting better and better!"

She threw her shoulders back, turned around and marched back up the stairs. Her Barry needed her!

***

The following Thursday, the Huckleberry Blue…Balls were celebrating in the lounge at Splitsville Lanes. Each team member wore the T-shirt Gracie had made up for them. It read "Huckleberry Blue Balls; oh get your mind out of the gutter!"

Gore in the *Garden*

"Here's to the second to last place finishers in the 'Mostly Over Forty League'," Mark said as he raised his glass.

Pauline took yet another large gulp of her beer and warbled her own toast. "Here's to not being over forty!"

Dave and Gracie laughed as Ted raised his glass. "Here's to old re-runs of Columbo!"

Gracie chimed in. "Here's to non-refundable deposits!"

There was a pause as everyone turned to look at Dave.

"Here's to beer!"

The entire lounge laughed at that toast.

The Huckleberry Blue…Balls began reviewing the latest murder in the town.

"One thing I don't understand," Pauline said, "Is why on earth Anita Frederickson killed Andrew Walters in the first place?"

Ted chuckled. "That woman does not know the meaning of self-incrimination. Even after being read her rights, she just kept talking. Before she married Barry, she worked for the City of Munson as an assistant in the urban planning department. She saw that Munson was negotiating with Huckleberry town council to appropriate part of the rural area where Andrew, Barb and Barry's houses sit."

"They want to build a honking condo development, complete with its own car dealership and shopping mall," Gracie added.

Ted nodded. "So Anita spent some time getting her car fixed at Barry's shop; and the next thing you know, they're married. Her masterplan was to kill Andrew, blame Barb, buy their properties and then sell all three and apparently retire in the Caribbean." He raised his bushy eyebrows. "Without Barry."

Pauline still look confused. "That's a long-range plan, to be sure. Did she really have the time to do all that before Munson City expanded?"

"Oh you bet!" Gracie claimed. "We don't even know if Munson City expansion is going to get the green light. Their so-called appropriation will be up for a serious discussion. The Huckleberry Town Council have a referendum planned for the fall." She stopped and looked serious. "And I need you all to vote no to this proposed expansion."

The team nodded while Pauline persisted. "So, what, she just phoned Andrew up and said come on over and I'll bash your head in for you?"

"That's the one thing she wasn't clear about. She hasn't told us what she said to Andrew to get him to walk over. But when he arrived, she had a mix master ready, one of their wedding presents, and just walked out and killed him."

Gracie squinted her eyes. "Was it a red mix master? I saw that on sale in January at Irene's Emporium. I was going to buy it, but when I went back; it was gone."

"It was indeed a red one," Ted acknowledged and added, "That's why she thought she had washed all the blood off, but she hadn't."

Gracie leaned forward and told the group. "And Barry was completely innocent in all this. Barb? Not so much."

Dave raised his hand. "Here's to beer, and of course, true love. My understanding is Barb hid the body in her pond because she was madly in love with Barry. I am madly in love with someone." He winked at Pauline, "but I would never hide a body in a pond for her." He took a drink. "If we had a pond."

Pauline patted Dave's hand. "Right back at you, Babe."

Mark ordered another round and picked up the story. "When Barb left Friday morning, we had already obtained the search warrant and drained her pond. She was arrested at the Court House for obstruction in a murder investigation."

Gore in the *Garden*

Ted continued. "Right. As you'll recall, Anita had drugged Barry, so when he awoke he dashed to the Court House to get the truth. When he did, his mind was blown. He actually allowed Barb to stand by him and pat his hand as we explained everything to him."

Pauline shook her head. "He must have been heartbroken. What did he do?"

Ted tented his fingers and tapped them together. "He posted bail." Here he paused dramatically then added, "For Barb."

Gracie, of course, already knew this, but the three officers who had been working other cases, choked and spit out their mouthful of beer.

Gracie raised her glass. "To finding true love, no matter how strange the journey!"

Ted winked at Gracie, "Or how many detours it takes!"

Shelley Dawn Siddall

Don't Be Koi With Me!

"Did you do something bad, but can't quite remember? Did your neighbor do something bad, and you want to get the goods on them? Contact Gracie Noseworthy Investigations at 555-2368. I sniff out trouble!"

Anderson Payne read the advertisement again.

She's got some nerve, he thought, I'm going over there right now and give her a piece of my mind. He was so angry he left his front door open as he exited and marched down the road.

He knocked on a cobalt blue door and thrust a newspaper into the face of the owner when she opened the door.

"You've got some nerve advertising when you are the worst neighbor in the world."

"Mr. Payne," Gracie said calmly, "Ever since you moved in one year ago, I have steadfastly refused to participate in any humorous endeavor concerning your surname. I'm now reconsidering that stand."

Anderson shook the newspaper again. "Your cats have been terrorizing my fish!" he proclaimed.

Gracie took a step back and looked at her two beautiful Sphynx cats, Zoey, and Frank, curled up together on the window seat in the sunlight.

"Perhaps in their dreams," she said. "Mr. Payne, my cats are indoor cats. They were rescue cats and have no desire to ever go outside again."

"They've been terrorizing my fish I tell you. I've followed them back here."

It was early in the morning and Gracie was still down a quart of coffee. She felt herself getting a bit snippy.

"No you didn't. I don't let my cats out. If you have one hundred dollars, you can hire me to track down these fish-terrorizing cats. A photograph or a video of these felines in action would be helpful. Otherwise, go home." From her height, she could stare down at him. She hoped she was being intimidating, as she was quite miffed.

"One is a big fluffy tabby and the other one is a small grey cat. Here, let me look at yours." Anderson Payne put one hand on the door and one foot on the threshold of Gracie's home.

Gracie clapped her hands together loudly in front of his face, narrowly missing his nose.

It startled him so much he stopped trying to barge his way in.

"You're fastly becoming a pain in the rear. For your information, the onus probandi or burden of proof is on you, Mr. Payne. But I'll repeat myself in case you didn't hear me the first time. I don't let my cats out. I don't even have a pet door! What I do have is toast and cream cheese on a plate in the kitchen waiting for me." She leaned her face close to Anderson's. "Now, what would be the appropriate thing to say to me at this juncture?"

"Good morning?" he asked.

"I was hoping for an apology, but that will have to do. A good morning to you as well, Mr. Payne in the rear."

Gracie quietly shut the door and returned to her breakfast.

Mr. Payne muttered to himself all the way home.

"Thinks she can just tune me out, does she? Thinks I don't know her cats are skulking around my fishpond? Drastic times call for drastic measures. She'll be sorry."

As he approached his house, a large fluffy tabby walked out his front door. It sat down on the step and waited for Anderson.

Anderson started running towards the tabby while yelling, "You stupid cat! I'm going to get you and return you to your mother, dead or alive!"

The cat, unperturbed, began a serious grooming routine which stopped Anderson in his tracks. He actually shuddered as he looked at the cat, hind leg stretched out, oblivious to the world.

Anderson inched by the cat and slammed his door. He threw the paper he was still clutching down on the kitchen table and went out the back door to his pond to check on his fish.

They were his jewels.

Last year, after he and his wife split, he bought this house on Landsbury Lane. The first thing he did was build a garden pond. A beautiful home fit for his treasures.

Then, he carefully selected the Koi he wanted. This time around he wanted personality. Anderson purchased two tea colored Chagoi Koi. He was in the process of teaching them to feed from his hand. Although they didn't have the more spectacular coloration of other types of Koi, they would swim up to greet him every time he came to the pond's edge.

He also purchased two Tancho Koi; each fish was a solid white with a single red dot on their head.

His ex-wife never understood his fascination with his pets.

"Anderson," she'd say, "Fish are cold and creepy like snakes. How on earth can they possibly be friendly?"

But she tolerated the fish and he tolerated her, until the pond heater tragedy. Anderson had to leave for a work project for a week and had left his wife specific instructions for the care of his fish.

Gore in the *Garden*

He really didn't expect that she would measure the length of his fish on a daily basis in order to determine the amount to feed them, so he estimated their daily protein pellet requirements and set out little packets for each day for her to, as she put it, 'dump in the pond'. Anderson also drilled into her that the aerator should always be running, along with the filter.

He pleaded with her to test the pH every day and showed her how easy it was. Lastly, he asked her to check the temperature of the water and make sure it stayed at eighteen degrees Fahrenheit.

She forgot pretty much everything Anderson reviewed with her until she was sitting in their house one night and found it a bit chilly. She turned up the furnace and settled back in on the couch with a romance novel when she finally thought of the fish. As Anderson was due home early the next morning she ran out to the shed and cranked up the heat in the pond. That deed done, she spent a delightful evening reading her bodice ripper and then fell asleep.

She awoke to the sound of Anderson screaming.

She had fried all the fish.

Although Anderson's Divorce lawyer repeatedly informed him that he could not charge his soon to be ex-wife with murder, Anderson inundated the police force in Munson with daily visits and phone calls. The police force in turn decided frequent visits to his home at inopportune times day and night were in order. Anderson finally got the message and let the matter drop, but he religiously read the paper cover to cover to see if any cases of animal cruelty had been reported. He hoped his former wife had learned her lesson, but by gum, he'd be there as a witness for the prosecution if he was ever needed.

He wasn't.

He sold his home, split the proceeds with his ex-wife Cynthia and moved to Huckleberry. But now his living ornaments; his only friends; his Koi, were being threatened by a different kind of wickedness.

Cats. Anderson hated cats. Unfortunately, they loved him. Probably because of the way he smelled. Regardless, they found him wherever he went and now, they had descended upon his home.

He had put non-toxic dye in his pond a few months ago to darken the water and thereby discourage predators, but it didn't help. That darn tabby and his little grey buddy would be at the pond's edge every morning, watching his fish.

The silly fish would come up and nibble at their paws and then the cats would strike, literally. They batted at the fish. It wouldn't be long, Anderson knew, before they tried to eat them. That's why he had to act!

The thing was, he didn't know what to do.

After he spent some time with his fish, Greg, Jan, Bobby, and Cindy, (even if he got another female, he would never have a Marcia; it sounded too much like Cynthia), he went back in the house, picked up the paper and read the flyer for the local hardware store.

They had live animal traps for feral cats on sale.

***

Ted brought a large mug of coffee to Gracie and set it on the table in front of her.

"What was that all about?"

Gracie held up her pointer finger, said, "Bear with," and had a great gulp of coffee.

"Crazy neighbor is absolutely convinced that my cats are terrorizing his fish. But on to more interesting subjects; did Julia Smith's husband ever show up? Trudy-Faye was by yesterday to

Gore in the *Garden*

inveigle me in being a food stop on the garden tour this year, and she went on and on about the bedposts and the marigolds."

Ted slathered more cream cheese on his toast.

"I know, we had a slew of missing persons reported this spring. Nothing new on the Smith front, although I must say, I love her garden beds. I don't suppose you've taken on any new clients?"

"Alas, no. My calendar is unfortunately open. This means the Huckleberry Police Force will have to solve this, wait, what do you mean a slew?"

Ted smiled. "No flies on you, Gracie my girl! Down at the Hospice, a Nurse didn't show up for work last night. I know you volunteer there when your demanding investigating work will allow…"

Gracie eyed her remaining piece of toast and debated throwing it at Ted.

"Who is missing and how do you know she's not just sick and forgot to phone in?" she said.

"Emma Bartlett. Both her co-workers and room-mate reported her missing."

"Why do people with the loveliest names turn out to be the nasty? You'd think that being bestowed with such a beautiful name like Emma, she would be a jewel of a girl." Gracie slapped the table. "Well, I'm here to tell she is not a jewel, more like a chunk of coal. I've seen her in action."

"Did you report her?" asked Ted, knowing Gracie was a staunch advocate for the elderly and vulnerable.

"You bet! Several times. She works at a Hospice, for heaven's sake. People are dying! If they want ice cream for breakfast, they can have it, yet I've heard Nurse Emma flatly refuse to bring the patient ice cream."

"And so you went to the kitchen yourself and…?" asked Ted, already knowing the answer.

"I brought Mr. Hiebert double the ice cream." Gracie sat up straighter. "I actually served it in two separate dishes; more for Emma to wash up."

"There should be a test," Ted said looking off in the distance.

"Yes," said Gracie, "At a certain age, say twenty, your actions should already be speaking to your character. A test at that age should be given to determine if you are worthy to carry the name you are born with." Gracie made check marks in the air.

"Kind to strangers? Check. Has a job and is good at it? Check. Loves cats? Check."

Ted chuckled. "What if they love dogs? Or even fish?"

Gracie considered this. "They would get half a point."

"And let's say they fail the beautiful name test. Let's say they are not worthy of the name Emma, or Madison or even Gracie?"

"Then their moniker is changed there and then to Hortense or Helga or if it's a boy, Harry or Herbert." Gracie poured them more coffee. "That way, people would know right off what sort of person they are!"

Ted added a heavy dollop of cream to his coffee. "Ah, but what about a leopard changing spots? You know, turning your life around and all that sort of goody two shoes nonsense. Then the name would again, be totally inappropriate to say nothing of setting up the bearer for pre-judgment."

Gracie thought about the point for a second. "I wouldn't mind a leopard named Helga," she said.

Ted smiled as a thunderous knocking on the front door began. He started to stand up when Gracie reminded him, "I don't need rescuing, thank you."

Anderson Payne, florid and panting, stood in the doorway. He held up the hardware store flyer.

"I'm buying a humane animal trap right now!" he shouted.

Gore in the *Garden*

Gracie walked outside, carefully shut the screen door as her two inquisitive roommates were suddenly awake. She leaned against the door frame.

"Oh Mr. Chronic Payne, I do wish you all the best with your future endeavors. Please, please come by again and let me know which model you've purchased."

Her neighbor looked confused. He shook his head and walked back to his car muttering under his breath the entire way.

Gracie waved politely as he drove off. Zoey and Frank continued to stare at the screen door for about five minutes, hoping the nice smelling man would return. When he didn't, they decided it had been a strenuous day already and another nap was in order.

***

Her name would be Marcia, Anderson thought disgustedly as he read the nametag of the cashier at the Hardware store. But she did smell good. He searched his memory for the scent. She smelled like rose water.

Marcia covered her mouth and giggled. She looked one way and then the other.

"Don't tell anyone, but I actually detest cats." She started to blush and giggled again.

Relieved at finding a kindred spirit, Anderson began to tell her about the horrors of finding the cats at the pond's edge.

"My females," he whined, "Are so stressed that they bleed from their gills."

Marcia felt like gagging, but instead simpered, "Oh the poor little fishies. Do you mind terribly if I ask their names?"

Anderson was elated and immediately opened his phone and showed Marcia photos of his Koi. "This big one is Greg, this is

Cindy, the spot on her head is just a little irregular and extends to her nostrils, so not really a show fish. This is Bobby and here is the jewel of the bunch, Jan. Just look at perfectly centered red mark. It doesn't touch Jan's eyes, nor the scales at her shoulders."

Marcia tittered again. "I'm afraid I don't know anything about fish. Are they terribly expensive?" Her voice got a little flatter. "What about this Jan, how much would she go for?"

"Oh I would never sell my Koi, but I suppose she would be worth around a grand. Her scalation and the brightness of her Tancho mark, well, her value could be even more!"

Marcia's eyes glittered. She used her high school girl voice again. "Oh how exciting. They must be so pretty to see in person."

***

Gracie had gone to the Hospice to snoop. She got a lot more than she bargained for. It seems everyone on staff had a horror story to tell about the missing Nurse, Emma Bartlett.

"Do you know, her narcotic count never balanced?" The RN, Jasmine Summan told Gracie. "Now, I shouldn't really be telling you this, but you're here so often, you're practically on staff, but Emma always had some excuse about the drugs always coming up short."

"Don't you have protocols in place for that sort of thing?" Gracie asked. Even though she was wearing her flats, she towered over the little strawberry blonde Jasmine. Now there was a gal worthy of her name.

"Oh we have the 'two staff to sign out narcotics' rule, but she just ignored it. I even tried to get a camera put in the medication room, but apparently it contravened privacy laws." Jasmine continued writing in the chart as she talked.

Gracie was always amazed at how Nurses could multi-task.

Jasmine continued, "She worked nights, you know, and had ever so many patients 'fall back asleep so they didn't need the shot after all'. The RN looked angry. "I haven't been able to pin anything on her yet. She says she just discards the needles in the sharps container and forgets to record everything."

"So do you think she is taking these ampoules of pain medications for her own personal use? I mean, could she be telling the truth about forgetting?" Gracie asked.

Jasmine stopped writing in the chart she was working on and looked heartbroken.

"The sad truth, Gracie, is I don't think she is telling the truth. I believe she is stealing from the patients. I've cross-checked the charts and do you know that every time Emma is on duty, there are notes from the Care Aides indicating uncontrolled pain for a lot of the patients. Families have gone to their Doctors to complain 'that the pain medicine isn't working anymore' and of course, the Doctor obliges and increases the dose."

The tall sliver haired lady covered her mouth with her hands. She looked horrified and wiped a tear from the corner of her eye.

"I've been here over night volunteering to keep a patient company and I've seen her be rude and neglectful to her patients…"

"Which you've reported and thank you for that," Jasmine said.

Gracie continued, "But I didn't know how bad it was. How low do you have to be to steal pain medication from dying people?"

The two women said at the same time, "Pretty damn low."

Gracie stood up, smoothed out imaginary creases in her slacks and thanked Jasmine for the talk and encouraged her to keep up the good work compiling evidence.

She needed some fresh air, so she headed out to the garden.

It was spectacular.

Shelley Dawn Siddall

Over the years, families of patients and patients themselves, had contributed to the beauty of the Hospice garden, which was in reality, several gardens. A large, tiled patio was safely under cover and hosted myriads of little bistro sets. From this starting point, several tiled paths, wide enough for wheelchairs, were lined by large hedges of Hansa roses. Each path led to a themed garden.

The largest by far was the vegetable garden. Gracie loved this area. It was made up of dozens of raised beds, built high enough for a person using a wheelchair to roll right up to the gardens' edge and begin cultivating. This garden was one of the more popular spots visited by patients and families alike. During a time in their lives when permanent change was encroaching, it gave each a sense of purpose and accomplishment.

As Gracie was fond of saying, "Hope is a seed planted." Hope that the loved one's passing would be peaceful and those left behind would eventually be able to find a new kind of normal.

Gracie returned to the patio which of course was adorned with flowers. Massive terracotta pots of red and white cascading petunias bejeweled the area along with hanging pots of ivy geraniums. Their trailing blossoms met the petunias and created stunning floral pillars.

As Gracie stood and admired the view, a robust voice to her right offered her a diversion.

"Want to run up those mountains with me? Bet I could beat you to the top!"

Gracie sat down beside the young woman with a patient wristband and introduced herself.

"Hi. I'm Gracie Noseworthy and I'm sure I would win. Let's do this thing!"

The young woman broke into hearty laughter.

"Most excellent! I'm Petra Kennedy. I'm an inmate, um, patient of this institution but you could probably tell by my buddy here." She pointed to the oxygen cylinder resting in her walker.

Gracie shrugged. "Many people carry oxygen. I'm sorry, I'm not buying your claim."

"Stage four melanoma and counting. Probably won't last the week."

"You're pretty chipper for someone who's going to be dead in a week. No, I'm sorry, you must be a visitor. Now about this race, when are we going to do it? I have openings in my schedule next week."

Petra Kennedy started to laugh again. "Finally, someone with a sense of humor! My entire family is all doom and gloom. I know they love me, but I want to live while I can!"

Gracie put her hand on Petra's. "So next week then? For our race?"

Petra gave her a hug, then started to laugh and cry at the same time.

"You know, the Doctor bumped up my meds after Nurse Bartlett did her usual trick, so I've feeling all sorts of wonderful one minute and then weepy the next. It's weird."

Gracie smiled tenderly. "It's normal in a weird situation. We're not given an instruction manual on how to act when we're dying. You're doing just fine. Now what is this trick that Nurse Bartlett does?"

"She claims she gives you the hydromorphone, but she doesn't. I would know if she gave me a shot in my arm. I'm a lepidopterist; I collect all sorts of butterflies." Petra scrunched up her shirt sleeve and showed Gracie the permanent port, called a butterfly, in her bicep for pain medicine.

"They change this every seven days. I guess they won't have to worry about next week," Petra said.

"Okay," Gracie said evenly. "What do you have planned for this week?"

"Besides training for our race?"

Both women laughed.

"I'm going to gather my family and tell each one of them the secrets I've kept from them my entire twenty-six years. Then I'm going to tell them all the secrets they've told me over the years about one another."

Gracie shifted in her chair and leaned towards her new friend. "Do you suppose I could come by and watch the fireworks?"

"Of course," Petra said as she lifted up the throw that covered her lower body. She was a double amputee. "But be sure to bring me a pair of running shoes. Pink ones!"

Gracie laughed. "You bet!"

***

No one but Anderson had lived in his home for over a year, yet it was surprisingly quiet when he returned with his trap. That woman, Marcia, had the most delightful tinkling laugh.

Plus, she wanted to see his fish. She asked to see his fish. This was remarkable. He brought the carton containing the feral cat trap out to his pond.

Bobby and Greg had already swam up to the edge, but it was Greg who ate out of Anderson's hand. A harbinger of good things to come no doubt.

In no time at all he had the cage built, which really made sense as he wrote instruction manuals for do-it-yourselfers to put furniture together. In fact, he had been honored at a recent convention hosted by the multi-national parent company.

He didn't go.

Gore in the *Garden*

After the water heater incident with Cynthia, he vowed he would never leave his home again, no matter how prestigious the award or how tempting the all-expenses paid international convention appeared.

Not. Going. To. Happen.

"I'll tell you what else is not going to happen," Anderson said aloud. "I am not going to bait this with fish. Oh no." He hung a large ball of catnip inside the cage after he had sprinkled some in a trail leading from the fence.

He carefully measured his fish, tested the pH and temperature, and did all the checks that made him and the fishies, quite comfortable. The duckweed even looked healthy and although the dye in the pond was dissipating, Anderson wasn't worried. He had the cage now. He went back inside his home and straight to his office. After checking the live feed monitoring his Koi, he settled down at his computer to work. Working from home was worth it. Every now and again, Anderson would look up from his screen and watch the fish undulating in their home.

The cage looked vulgar on the otherwise serene scene, but he hoped it would only be temporary.

***

Marcia knew her new romance would only be temporary. She liked temporary liaisons. Working at the hardware store was a great way to meet men.

She normally went after married men, but this fish man, what was his name again? Marcia checked the receipts. Right. Anderson Payne on Landsbury Lane. Okay, she had it locked in. All she had to do was drop by, scoop up a fish and make a couple hundred bucks or more. It depended how fast her fence could move a fish.

And speaking of fish, Anderson had been easy to reel in.

Shelley Dawn Siddall

Behind Marcia's contrived vacant stare lurked a cunning brain. When Anderson started nattering on about his Koi, Marcia correctly assumed that he was a fan of Japanese culture and quickly adopted a flirtatious but modest manner. Of course it was stereotypical, but she figured he would fall for her act. He did. The more she was self-effacing, the more Anderson went on about his fish.

She remembered a particularly nauseating phrase he had uttered.

"When you come over to see my Koi, the whole bunch will be at my home with the exception of one. I'll have Greg, Marcia, Jan, Bobby, and Cindy. The only one I'll need is, dare I say it, Peter."

At the time, Marcia felt her lip curling. How dare he compare her to a fish! She pushed down her anger, covered her mouth again and giggled. She had her routine down pat. Gain the mark's confidence, strike, then blackmail.

This Anderson she wouldn't even have to sleep with.

Marcia had made that particular maneuver not a few times in the past. A calculated ploy to entrap married men. Sure, they still shopped at Huckleberry Hardware, but studiously avoided her checkout. Marcia went out of her way, though, to make eye contact with them. Her raised eyebrow ensured the next month's blackmail payment would definitely arrive.

On her break, she phoned her fence. He said it would be tricky, but he would buy the fish for three hundred. She countered with eight; they settled on five.

Marcia already had enough money for the trip of her dreams. She mentally reviewed her itinerary as she watched the clock, waiting for her boring shift to end. First to Madrid to loiter in the 1960's Futurism airport then out to the street to view the murals and eat oxtail stew in phyllo pastry. Then on to Morocco to the Dar Menebhi Palace in Marrakech to wander in the art museum located there.

Gore in the *Garden*

A customer interrupted her musings. After he left, Marcia slowly closed the cash drawer. Yes, she had enough money for her travels, she just wanted more. She planned to stay in the swankiest hotels.

"Enough of this noise!" she said, taking off her apron and dumping it on the counter. She grabbed her purse and walked out of the store. At this point, she didn't care about burning bridges.

Getting into Anderson Payne's backyard was easier than she had anticipated. She merely reached over, lifted the latch, and walked in. She failed to see the numerous cameras set up.

A lovely orange tabby followed her in.

"Oh hello darling," she said as she scratched it's head. She actually loved cats. The cat began purring mightily but suddenly took off like a shot. Marcia shrugged. I've got work to do, she thought. I'll buy a dozen cats later if I want to.

She placed the large duffel bag she had brought on the ground and pulled out an industrial strength plastic bag. Her plan was simple. Catch the fish, put it in the bag with some water and phone Terry, her fence, to pick up the goods. She might even catch two fish as long as she was here.

Marcia figured Anderson would have a net handy and found it easily. For the first time, she looked in the pond. Despite the elaborate schemes she had hatched in the past, she really didn't research this one. Her greed for a quick buck made her careless.

"Crap," Marcia said. The fish were a lot bigger than she had anticipated. Perhaps she would just take one then. There were a couple of basic brown ones that had come right up to the edge of the pond; but not the one she was looking for. She needed a white one, with a red mark on its head.

Marcia inched forward, searching for her prey, while both toes of her sneakers soaked up water. She saw a shimmer of white in the water and stretched out her hand holding the net.

The clang of the cat trap door as it slammed shut startled her. She lost her balance and fell in the pond. The long handle of the net wedged into the underwater alcove Anderson had built for his Koi, (so they could have a little shade in the hot summer months) and effectively trapped the con artist.

All Marcia had to do was to let go of the pole, but she was determined to get that fish. She tried to pull the handle from the rock while the mesh of the net was ensnared on her cutesy flower barrettes.

As Marcia twisted in the water the net tightened around her head. After a while, she stopped twisting. The Koi inspected her for protein pellets, but finding none, moved to the opposite side of the pond. They wanted nothing to do with this stranger that had barged into their home and interrupted their peaceful gliding.

***

Anderson was more productive that afternoon then he had been for a long time. His mind was no longer burdened by the threat to his Koi. He had acted! He even had a date planned, which he really didn't want to think about. Too messy.

He wrote on, adding diagrams and explanations to the instruction sheets. Several completed sheets later, Anderson did something very uncharacteristic. He took a nap. Before he went to lay down on his couch, Anderson checked his live feed on the pond including the underwater camera. Everything was in order. The males were swimming faster than the graceful females, but that was normal. The cat trap was still empty, but it was early days yet.

He slept. He had many dreams that afternoon. At one point, a jail cell clanged shut on the boys who had tormented him in school. He partially woke up, said 'it's okay, Mother, they can't hurt me

Gore in the *Garden*

now' and rolled over. He dreamt of ribbons and gold stars and hang-gliding over rivers of molten lava.

As he was to tell the police later, it wasn't until his alarm went off on his watch that he woke up. It was time to feed his fish, so he went out to the pond without checking the monitors.

The first thing he noticed was the tabby caught in the cage. It sat up when it saw Anderson and began purring and rubbing it's body against the bars.

He was overjoyed! He'd drop this cat off at the pound and hopefully catch the little grey one next.

Anderson raised his eyes to the pond and couldn't quite understand what he was seeing. It was a pair of sneakers, but the soles of the sneakers. And there seemed to be legs underneath them.

He called 911.

Anderson was very panicky when Constable Pauline had to climb in the water to release the handle of the net that was holding the body down. The two officers wouldn't let him go near the pond despite his protestations that he had to keep his fish calm.

In fact, Anderson was so discombobulated that he dropped down beside the cage and aimlessly patted the cat.

Pauline cut the net from Marcia's head and with Constable Dave's help, dragged the body out of the pond.

"She's only been in there, what, three hours, but she sure is white!" Dave said.

Pauline couldn't help herself. "Fish belly white," she snickered.

***

Anderson made several solemn vows that evening after he brought the cat to the pound. One, no napping in the afternoon.

Two, no females at his house, ever, unless they were Gracie Noseworthy.

He had revised his opinion of her when he saw her at the pound, looking over the latest batch of rescued animals. Anderson was ready to go and triumphantly announce he had caught one of her cats, when a worker pointed out Gracie.

"Yes, I know who she is," said Anderson tersely.

"Do you know that she adopted two sphynx cats a few years ago and every time new cats or kittens come in, she works hard to find homes for them?"

Anderson frowned. "What are Sphynx cats?"

The worker called up a photo and showed Anderson. "They're hairless cats. Gracie breaks out in hives if she touches animals with hair."

Anderson wanted to crawl in a hole and die. He cringed when he thought of how he had yelled at Gracie that day. Twice.

At that moment, Gracie caught sight of him and waved. She walked up to him and put her hand on his shoulder.

"My friend Ted Bailey, a Detective Sergeant on the HPD, told me all about the trouble at your home today. I'm so sorry to hear that your fish were endangered. How are they now?"

Anderson blushed at her kindness and mumbled something about returning to normal. He drove home with his empty cage and began making his vows. When he reached the third vow, he spoke aloud.

"Three. No dating ever, no matter how much they say they love fish." He relented a little, amending the last vow. "Not unless they have their own Koi pond and are independently wealthy."

Once the police returned his videos, Anderson watched in morbid fascination the events that happened while he was sleeping.

From time to time, when the loneliness threatened to overtake him, he would watch the videos again.

Gore in the *Garden*

He especially liked the view from the underwater camera.

Shelley Dawn Siddall

How To Refuse An Offer

Fred Downton carefully moved the curtain on his kitchen door and peeked into his garage.

Damn. His car hadn't made it home last night. He had no idea where it might be because he normally didn't drive anywhere. Clearly, the car had run away from home.

Fred was a confirmed homebody. Some, like his cop buddy Mark, even called him a hermit. He had his groceries delivered along with his cases of vodka.

Needless to say his recollection of last night was a little fuzzy. His recollection of most of his nights was fuzzy.

But last night was different, he could just feel it. There was something important he was forgetting. Something he had done or had to do; his killer hangover was preventing him from getting a handle on things.

He could hear his neighbor dutifully mowing his lawn.

Fred thought hard. I better go mow my lawn, he thought, I mean, what would the neighbor's think of me if I let my place go to rack and ruin? He found his wrap-around sunglasses and headed out to the back yard where his electric mower waited in the half that was covered with grass. A garden comprised the other half, with a large compost pile in the corner.

Gore in the *Garden*

He looked over at the compost pile for a while. Something, something was niggling at him.

Nope. He couldn't remember. His neighbor waved at him, and Fred carefully waved back and attempted a smile. Even his face hurt. He stopped trying to smile, took a deep breath and turned on his lawnmower.

The sound and vibration was worse than he had anticipated. He closed his eyes and pushed. It was important to Fred to keep up appearances even if he died trying.

Fred was stuck with the electric mower because the smell of gas made him nauseous. He had no desire to drive to the gas station and fill up a container. Plus, he could never remember to charge the battery for his other mower that had sat in his shed for years.

Suddenly it occurred to Fred that he might run over the cord if he didn't open his eyes.

He had opened his eyes just in time. He idled the mower and flipped the cord out of the way. The motion seemed to replay several times, so he stood until his equilibrium was reestablished. A large grasshopper lay in the direct path of the machine.

"Move," Fred whispered hoarsely.

The grasshopper declined to give up his patch of grass. Unwisely, Fred decided to flick the grasshopper out of the way with the cord. Again Fred remained motionless for a few seconds. He kicked at the insect with his sockless lace-less sneaker.

There was a direct correlation between the intensity of Fred's hangover to his degree of frustration. Fred flew into a murderous rage, ramped up his lawnmower and ran over the grasshopper.

He also ran over the cord.

He kicked the lawn mower and for some reason, felt impelled to walk back to his house on the only strip of grass he had just cut. It looped gently to his back stairs. He climbed up and walked into the screen door that was plastered with warning plastic butterflies.

As Fred gingerly touched his nose, he decided he needed a drink. His tongue kept sticking to the roof of his mouth. A good wholesome drink of orange juice would help.

He nearly walked into the screen door again, but at the last minute opened the glass door and walked to the fridge and retrieved a carton of orange juice and poured himself a drink. It didn't taste how it normally did. Maybe it had gone off he wondered. He checked the date. Nope, it was fine.

As he attempted to drink the juice, his gaze landed upon his kitchen cupboards. Fred frowned and carefully tilted his head to look at the top of the cupboards where his vintage tin containers usually sat. They weren't there now.

Fred still clinging to the half empty glass, carefully shut the screen door, and walked out of the kitchen leaving the fridge door open and the carton on the counter.

Did he ever have vintage tins gracing the top of his cupboards?

A piercing siren sounded. Fred flung out his arms, threw the glass down and covered his ears.

"Make it stop!" he pleaded.

It was his phone playing a custom ring tone.

"I gotta tell you, you were pretty convincing last night Freddy old pal, old buckaroo. We tromped all over your hell's half acre searching for your latest victim."

It was his cop buddy Mark LeClair checking in on him.

"Heah Mark," Fred managed to say. He picked up the now empty glass and a bunch of papers from the floor. They were all covered with Fred's elegant long hand. Bits and pieces of stories he had started and never finished.

Orange juice was still flowing over his notes. Fred was able to read a line 'it looked like murder to me' before he blotted it with the backs of even more notes.

Mark had been talking to him the whole time.

Gore in the *Garden*

"Last night, my work computer warned me that I had a mandatory password reset but I couldn't do it early. So I had to come in and change my password this morning. Apparently the police computer system doesn't care if it's your day off or not. If I didn't change it today, I would be locked out." He was concerned by the continued silence on Fred's end of the phone. "Say buddy, have you eaten today?"

Fred was still picking paperwork off the floor. A juice covered manuscript caught his attention and he gingerly bent down and picked it up.

"Did I write this?" he muttered.

"Oh good, you're writing again. Way to go buddy!"

The hungover grasshopper murderer flipped to the last page and read the Author's name and winced.

"Byron Eggplant? Please tell me I did not chose that as my new pen name!"

Mark did some quick typing.

"No worries Fred, it's the name of a guy who has recently published one eBook on Kindle. The book is called "How to stand out from the crowd by choosing a unique pen name like Byron Eggplant." Mark clicked on a link. "Okay, it's not you. I'm on his Author Central page and this guy is very slight and looks like he's fourteen. Not you in the least."

"Thanks Mark. In one fell swoop, you have reminded me that I haven't been able to publish in years, I'm overweight and middle-aged."

Mark did some more typing on his computer.

"You're still way above him in rankings. Don't worry, you'll write your next best seller yet. I have faith in you. I'll be by with donuts soon."

The middle-aged author went over to his couch. He thought it might be best if he just curled up and died. He began to remove the blanket from the couch when he felt resistance. He tugged a little harder and heard a ripping sound.

With the blanket removed, a stain the length of the couch was revealed. It was very dark, almost brownish.

"Please tell me I did not kill someone!" Fred said.

But the evidence was there. A large blood stain on the couch, and after a quick search, pools of blood congealed on the hardwood floor.

The rocking chair was far too dangerous with the current state of his equilibrium, so he chose the recliner. He dozed there until Mark used his key and came in with donuts.

"Basic glazed for you and apple fritters for me," Mark said as he searched for a place to sit. He looked at the couch and then followed the pools of blood to the back door.

"Well these have all dried. We offered to clean this up last night you know, but you said you would do it. Now you've really got a mess. Getting dried blood out of a couch; I don't think steam cleaning is going to do it. You might have to throw that one away."

The pistons in Fred's brain were barely firing, but he knew enough to realize he should say as little as possible.

"Thanks for the donuts Mark."

Mark was in the kitchen looking at the top of the cupboards.

"Yup," he said, "That must have been one doozy of a nosebleed. Why, you even have some blood up here. Dave and I couldn't figure out what you were doing, but at least we put the ladder away so you wouldn't fall off it again. How's the leg?"

"Nosebleed," said Fred relieved. Nothing was in the old memory bank, so he ate his donut and kept his mouth shut.

After Mark put on the coffee, he sat on the rocker and ate a couple of apple fritters in quick succession.

"You gave Dave and I a real run for our money last night. While we all appreciate your calls to the police station each night; you do get effusive with your praise, last night you were particularly desperate. Absolutely convinced you killed somebody."

"Do. Not. Rock," Fred croaked.

"Oh right. Sorry buddy. Let me get you a coffee."

The pain above Fred's left eye started to disappear with each gulp of coffee. Unfortunately, the mists refused to clear as Mark kept talking.

"It was a quiet night anyhow, so we thought we may as well pay you a visit. After we got you up from the floor, you insisted we walk out to the garden because you had buried a body there. You know what we found?"

Fred shook his head and immediately regretted it.

"Your vintage tins! For some reason, you buried them in amongst your potatoes." Mark started to laugh. "Do you know Fred; you literally have half your potatoes hoed?"

"Again, thank you for the age reminder."

"It was the silliest thing I had ever seen. I mean, I know you're a famous author and you have a creative mind, but to see old candy tins and what not sticking up out of the dirt! And the thing was, you spaced them so nice and evenly. Dave was amazed at that, because you could barely put one foot in front of the other. Man, you were plastered!"

The hungover author started to say, "It was for…" but his cop buddy interrupted him.

"I know, I know, it was for a story you're working on. Yup. You say that every night." Mark's face grew serious. "Now Fred, we don't mind you phoning us and bouncing murder ideas off us but calling us out is another matter. This time, we could indicate on our report that you had fallen and couldn't get up…"

Fred groaned at that line as the image of the old commercial came to mind. *Am I really that decrepit?*

"Sorry Mark. I'll try to contain my creativity like I have for the past eight years."

Fred Downton had exploded on the literary scene over eight years ago with his first novel, "Grandma's House". Those that picked it up thinking it was going to be a sweet memoir about apple pie and an apple-cheeked grannie, were initially horrified at the contents. Then fascinated.

It was a work of fiction written as a depiction of the inner workings of an all-female drug and alcohol treatment center. The book opened with a court room scene. A sixtyish woman was on the stand and a group of young women in the gallery were yelling "We love you Grandma!" Flashback scenes reveal that they were all current patients of the treatment center and that there was no love lost between them. The young women were being paid and or blackmailed to support the 'Grandma', who is charged with vehicular manslaughter of a child and has no recollection of the event. Nor does she have any empathy for the parents.

The book went on to detail the financial and political machinations of the Director and Counsellors of the treatment center, along with the sordid life stories of each of the women and their twisted interactions.

It was an immediate best seller. Fred still lived on the royalties, albeit dwindling royalties.

He had not been able to write anything since. Sure, he wrote bits and pieces of scenes but the major impediment to writing another best seller was that he didn't know how he wrote the first one.

He just couldn't remember.

In his more lucid moments he knew the blackouts from his drinking quite likely had something to do with his writer's block. Then he'd start to chuckle. The guy who had never stepped inside a drug and alcohol treatment center and who really needed to, had imagined a realistic pressure cooker. He knew it was somewhat realistic by the number of people who tried to sue him for exposing their stories.

They were unsuccessful but the publicity surrounding the libel suits brought against him and his publisher made the book even more notorious and thus more popular.

Which added even more pressure on Fred to write another book.

He couldn't.

Mark gently patted him on the shoulder and said, "Don't worry Fred. You'll get there. You'll find the words; I mean look at all this writing you've done! There's got to be something you can use in there." Mark walked to the front door, but then picked up a newspaper off the stair.

"I forgot; got this for you."

He threw it at Fred.

His reaction time delayed by his hangover, Fred's right hand went up and closed in the air.

The paper hit Fred full in the face.

After Mark left, Fred drank another cup of coffee, read the paper, and then decided to go through his bits and pieces of stories. Maybe Mark was right. Maybe there was something that would spark his imagination and he would go on a writing frenzy and be so immersed in the story; he wouldn't stop until it was done!

When he found a wallet belonging to Byron Eggplant underneath his notes, he started to worry. Especially since said wallet was covered in blood.

Fred picked up the newspaper. He had seen an advertisement he wanted to read again.

***

Shelley Dawn Siddall

Gracie Noseworthy re-read the ad she had run for months in the local newspaper:

"Did you do something bad, but can't quite remember? Did your neighbor do something bad, and you want to get the goods on them? Contact Gracie Noseworthy Investigations at 555-2368. I sniff out trouble!"

She pursed her lips and showed the ad to her cats.
"What do you think? Does it need sprucing up?"
Zoey and Frank stopped playing in the laundry basket and sat down on the clean towels they had been 'helping' to unfold. In their opinion, towels should never be folded, clean or not.
They stared at their human. If she wanted them to come in as consultants, clearly treats needed to be involved.
Gracie walked to the cat treat cupboard and was just about to remove the cat proof locking system, when her phone rang.
"Gracie Noseworthy speaking."
"This is Fred Downton at 3517 Springer Lane. I just read your ad and it seems to fit me. Can you help me?"
Gracie grinned at her cats who looked pointedly at the treat cupboard then back at her.
"Certainly. Has your neighbor done something bad, or is it you?"
"I'm pretty sure it's me. I think I killed somebody last night."
Gracie had to assess the degree of danger and so asked, "Are you looking at the body now? If so, how were they killed?"
She heard Fred sigh.
"I drink. I don't remember things. I found a bloody wallet and a headband. No matter how drunk I was, I don't think I would ever wear a headband."

Gracie shuddered. Who would? Even in the seventies, she loathed the things. She did a quick search on her phone and then returned to the call.

"I can come over now if that suits. Do not attempt to clean up. I want to see everything exactly as it was last night."

***

"Well I have heard of a technique that may access your memories," Gracie said as she perched on the edge of a rocker.

"Oh I'm not into hypnosis," Fred stated, "I'm pretty much a master of altering my conscious state. I've been known to be in a trance for days." He smiled for the first time that day.

The woman sitting opposite smiled back. She was older, but quite striking looking. Tall and slim, with long silver hair pulled back into a ponytail, she exuded confidence.

He liked her. She had come right over, looked at the blood evidence and wallet and expressed her concerns honestly.

"If the police didn't find anything, I'm sure I won't. I think I should give you back your check."

Fred begged her to try. He had been having little memory flashes. They weren't good.

She went on to explain. "It's not really a technique, more of a crazy theory that posits the memories acquired while you were, ahem, in your altered state, are locked away when you're sober."

He was disappointed and said sarcastically, "This I know."

Gracie ignored the sarcasm and continued.

"In order to access the memories, you must return to the former altered state. More simply put, let's get you as loaded as you were last night and see what you remember!"

Fred looked at the donut box Mark had brought. "Well, I've already had my breakfast. I could use a drink or two."

"No," insisted Gracie, "Not two. How many would you say you had last night?"

He walked over to his china cabinet and pulled out five cut crystal glasses. As he filled each with two shots of vodka and a lesser measure of orange juice he noted, "Yeah. They're lead crystal, but If I'm a murderer, that's the least of my problems."

"Good point," Gracie agreed. "Now what were you doing? Listening to music? Watching television? We want to re-create the atmosphere as close as possible."

Fred closed his eyes as he sipped his drink. Finally the orange juice, although warm, tasted right. His eyes flew open.

"I have a memory of standing over this Eggplant guy and telling him I'm going to kill him."

"Steady on. Let's approach this slowly. What do you normally do at night?"

Fred shrugged. "I sing loudly and poorly to my classic rock 'n roll albums while writing." He finished his drink and grabbed another. "You see, my last book was not genre specific. It was a little bit psychological thriller, a bit murder mystery, a bit of a cookbook…"

Gracie sat up even straighter with a bemused grin. "Cookbook?"

Fred laughed. "Yup. For some reason, I added an appendix with all the meals that were served at the treatment center."

Gracie was intrigued. She had heard of the book, but at the time, had a family member with their own addiction crisis and couldn't handle anyone else's drama, even if it was fictional.

She also noted, that with each drink, Fred was becoming more animated and oddly enough, more coordinated. He was pacing as he spoke, picking up books, empty pizza boxes and pens and putting them in their proper places. He also picked up quite a few articles of clothing.

Gore in the *Garden*

Fred was talking excitedly about his new book as he held the bundle of clothes.

"So I'm going to stay in one lane: psychological thriller all the way. This one is about a serial killer who actually interviews other serial killers because…" He paused. "The little twerp actually came to my door to interview me!"

Fred dropped the clothes on the couch and grabbed the bloody wallet off the coffee table and quickly found a piece of photo id.

"This is the guy. This is a genuine memory Gracie. I was belting out a song with Bob Seger, when this guy came to my front door."

Gracie was starting to unpack the lunch she had brought but motioned for him to continue.

"I took an immediate dislike to him." Fred had one hand on his hip while he pinched the bridge of his nose with the other.

"Not only was he wearing a head band, but he was also wearing a full-on seventies jazzercize outfit. It was hideous."

"I can well imagine," said Gracie as she munched her radishes. She was surprised and delighted that this crazy theory was working in practice.

"Needless to say, I intended to shut down the discussion forthwith, but the little idiot began flattering me. Yes, he quoted lengthy passages from my book and asked me all about the motivation of my characters." Fred hung his head. "I invited him in."

This was too good, Gracie thought, better than a movie. She kept crunching, absolutely fascinated as Fred drank more and more and remembered more and more. Unfortunately, the raw veggies just weren't doing it for her. She went to the dining room table and opened the donut box.

"Do you mind?" she asked.

"Go right ahead. Now then, where was I? Oh yes. This Byron Eggplant was and hopefully still is, quite the fanboy. After I signed his copy of "Grandma's House" and discussed at length the motivations of the main characters, he made the fatal error of asking me what my process was." Fred put his hands on his hips. "Well, I had no idea and I told him so. He was, shall we say, not amused. He continually pestered me. I think that may be why I killed him."

"It certainly seems a reasonable justification," Gracie said, "But let's not make that determination just yet. He irritated you. You were frustrated. He insisted and you…?"

"Killed him," Fred said defeated.

Gracie stood up and went to the fridge. "Clearly five is not your number. Start pouring the vodka Fred!"

***

It was several hours later. Fred had taken several trips down memory lane, but they were all the wrong lane. He spoke of pets, long gone, parents and friends, all gone. He took a nap.

Gracie spent the time surfing the web. In an effort to get to know her client better, she read back articles including the glowing reviews of his book and then, the disappointment about the delay of his follow-up novel. The disappointment turned into scathing personal attacks.

Gracie really felt that Fred had gotten a raw deal.

Fred finally awoke with a start insisting that there was a horse and a guy selling clothes for hundreds of dollars.

"I don't have that kind of money!" Fred cried. He looked at Gracie and slapped his knee. "Maybe if I had taken him up on his offer, I might be on my way to my next million-dollar best seller." Fred shook his head and chuckled. "Hire a personal assistant? What would I need with a personal assistant?" With a wide swing of his arm he encouraged Gracie to look at his life.

His life was basically condensed into that one room. Fred picked up his donut box, his remote control and one half of a pair of work socks.

"Food, entertainment and comfort! All within arm's reach. What more do I need?" he asked seriously.

Gracie nodded.

"And yet," Fred added, "That twerp in his purple and black spandex told me he could get my life back on track, starting with an interview showing 'the heart and soul of the real Fred Downton and his continued downward spiral into alcoholism and isolation from all human contact." Fred sniffed. "As if!"

Gracie felt a small sense of excitement. Could she steer the conversation? "And then he flattered you, you invited him in, you talked motivations and then…"

"Well then I wanted proof that my life would be better, artistically better, by hiring him." Fred stopped and rubbed his right hand. "I hit him at some point and gave him a bloody nose. Not entirely sure why, but it didn't stop him from trying to get my creative juices flowing."

Without warning, Fred ran out to the kitchen. Gracie followed and saw Fred grab a step stool and climb up. He ran his hands along the top of the cupboards.

"Ah ha!" Fred yelled and turned around with a gun in his hand.

Gracie's hand patted her jean jacket pocket. Yes, her cell phone was there. She might have to phone Ted, but not just yet.

"This Byron Eggplant put this in my face. Scared the daylights out of me let me tell you! I think that's why I punched him. Then he did this." Fred pointed the gun at Gracie and pulled the trigger.

It was a water pistol.

"Why on earth would he have done that?" Gracie demanded.

Fred climbed down the step stool with a remarkable quickness and went over to his dining room table, covered with his notes.

"It was supposed to impress upon me how fleeting life is, and I really should do something with mine. So I got the point and started to write."

He searched through and found a large purple spiral notebook and showed it to Gracie.

"What color would you say this is?"

Gracie rolled her eyes. "Eggplant purple would be my first guess, or rather aubergine!"

Fred tapped his nose. "Exactly. Everything that Byron had was purple. Anyhow, he said I should write in this while he went and prepared another motivating exercise for me." Fred stopped and looked into space remembering. "I really did get in the zone."

He started to flip through the notebook, but Gracie grabbed it from him.

"And then you went onto the next item, which was?"

"He put all my vintage tins in the garden. I do not know what in the hell his point was, but I was furious!"

Fred started twisting his head back and forth like a pug. He blinked his eyes as he started to really remember.

"This is good," Gracie said. "You were mad. Your precious tins were stuck in the dirt. Then what?"

"Then I may have killed him."

Gracie dropped her shoulders. "Ah shoot," she said.

Fred held up his index finger. "But then, maybe not. He was a nervous fellow, always moving. As we stood in the garden, I put my hands on his shoulders and told him to stop. I yelled at him and told him not until hell freezes over would I ever hire him. He was nuts and I would be nuts to accept his offer to be my assistant. I told him I refuse your offer completely."

Then Fred did something completely out of character. He gave Gracie a full toothy smile. He looked almost saintly.

Gore in the *Garden*

"Don't you get it?" he asked Gracie. "I said, I refuse your offer. I know where he is. Follow me."

As Fred headed out the back door, it was still light enough to see the one swath he had cut with the lawnmower. This time he did not feel compelled to walk on it but tromped ahead into the garden. He picked up a vintage tin, gently wiped off the dirt, then placed it back on the ground.

Gracie followed closely as Fred headed to the compost pile.

"See," Fred said excitedly, "I figured he belonged in the refuse pile because I refused his offer."

"Worst play on words ever," Gracie muttered while holding her breath. Actually, it wasn't because of the compost pile; it didn't smell that bad. Gracie was holding her breath because she hoped Mr. Byron Eggplant would be found and would be alive and this job would be over.

She figured she had put in enough hours to justify charging the full one hundred dollars and would head home if the fanboy wasn't found.

Fred took the cover off the compost pile and he and Gracie peered in.

There was Byron Eggplant's head. Fred slapped it.

"Well howdy stranger!" Byron said. He started to wriggle in the compost. Fred sighed and helped him out.

***

"Best sleep ever!" Byron enthused as he walked down the hallway to the front room where Gracie and Fred were both drinking coffee. Byron was wearing some of Fred's clothes after his shower.

"Once you dumped me in the compost pile and I couldn't get out, I felt overcome by emotion. I realized there I was, in the middle of the night, getting a warm hug by Mother Earth. What else did I need? So I drifted off to sleep with the sounds of the crickets."

"Oh. My. God." Fred said as he put down the spiral notebook.

"My thoughts exactly," Gracie added.

"Well yeah, Byron you're nuts, but this story. This is a really good outline for a novel!" Fred said happily. "I can't believe I'm saying this, but Byron, you're hired!"

Byron pretended to swoon but looked at the rest of the couch he had sat on and decided against swooning for the time being.

"Do you hear that?" Gracie asked, "I distinctly hear a cracking sound."

Fred smiled another huge grin. "Like hell freezing over? Sure I hear it too."

What no one in the room heard was a *plop*. A grasshopper hopped in through the open door and into Fred's neglected drink of vodka and orange juice with a loud plop.

Fred never drank another screwdriver in his life. The grasshopper, regrettably, was screwed.

Gore in the *Garden*

Canoodling in the Carnations

"I really don't care what Trudy-Faye says, I'm serving soup!" Gracie informed Pauline.

Her bowling buddy and one of the local police officers, looked up from her computer screen. "Could you serve some sort of cold soup? It's supposed to be hotter than blazes this week."

Gracie smirked. "Actually, that was my plan all along. Vichyssoise and Gazpacho. Trudy-Faye just assumed I'd be serving hot soup to the folks on the garden tour. I do enjoy Trudy-Faye's assumptions though. She gets so angry; it turns her face such a pretty shade of red."

"More of a magenta, I'd say," Pauline pondered as she finished her report. "There, the follow-up is done for that missing Nurse, Emma Bartlett. Nothing new to report. No bank activity, no credit card activity, no sightings, no cards, no letters, no nothing."

"What about her roommate? What has she been doing with her life since Emma disappeared?"

"Interestingly, she's got herself a new roommate. A man who used to be Emma's boyfriend," Pauline raised her eyebrows, shook her shoulders and said, "Hubba-hubba!"

"That is peculiar. One of my friends at the Hospice said that Nurse Emma and her boyfriend made good use of the gazebo on the Hospice grounds. He sure moved on fast; she really hasn't been missing for that long."

"Here's something else that's peculiar," Pauline said, "She's got a healthy, and I mean healthy balance in her bank account."

"On a Nurse's salary?" Gracie frowned. "So, we're thinking she's dead then?"

"Oh yeah," Pauline said. "No one decides to run away and leave over thirty grand behind!"

"Thirty grand? I wonder how she saved all that?"

Pauline leaned forward and said in a quieter voice to Gracie, "Well, I really shouldn't be telling you this, but…"

"So then you really shouldn't continue that sentence," said a stern voice behind Gracie.

Gracie rolled her eyes. "Ted, you are such a kill-joy. Just when Pauline was getting to the good part."

Ted smiled. "A very good afternoon to you too, Gracie. What brings you by the station?"

"Pauline and I are just going over the menu for the food stop at my place on the garden tour. She's going to help me serve, as long as she can have as many pieces of fudge as she wants."

"And have cuddles with the kitties," Pauline quickly added. "How are Zoey and Frank?"

Ted answered. "Oh just up to stuff and nonsense. You should have seen Zoey this morning! She was batting my sock around the bedroom like nobody's business." The Detective Sergeant suddenly stopped talking, turned red and walked quickly into his office and shut the door.

Pauline snickered and looked at Gracie. "I guess the cat's out of the bag now," she said.

**

Gore in the *Garden*

Gracie was still smiling when she drove home. Among their close friends, the relationship between her and Ted wasn't a secret, but he still felt uneasy with the whole concept of 'friends with benefits'. Ted thought they should get married. Gracie thought they should not.

Zoey and Frank didn't care either way, but they were curious about the large package Gracie brought in the house.

It was from Petra Kennedy, a Hospice patient who had died about two months previous. Inside the cardboard box was a pair of pink runners and a sealed letter.

Gracie fortified herself with a rum and coke and opened the letter. A clipping from the local newspaper fell out. It was Gracie's advertisement:

"Did you do something bad, but can't quite remember? Did your neighbor do something bad, and you want to get the goods on them? Contact Gracie Noseworthy Investigations at 555-2368. I sniff out trouble!"

"Dear Gracie," the letter read, "I didn't know you were *that* Gracie from the newspaper. You just told me you were retired from retail and had a small business that kept life interesting. It wasn't until I looked up your address that I found out you were a private investigator.

"No wonder you were so interesting to talk to.

"I really enjoyed our visits. Like I said when we first met, my family, although they love me to bits, are all doom and gloom. You and I could talk about my impending death without drama and then have a rum and coke and just plain gossip about everybody.

"You're probably wondering how you got this letter and the shoes. I had my Mom promise to mail this stuff to you after I died. And promise not to read this letter. I don't think she did because she certainly would have freaked out.

"You just dropped off my wonderful pink runners and now I'm returning them. I'll tell you why later. But remember how I said I was going to sit my family down and spill all the secrets they didn't know about me and didn't know about each other?"

"I had a change of heart after I revealed my first secret to my Mom. I told her I had started smoking at fourteen not sixteen like she thought. Well, she started crying and blaming herself for not stopping me. She went on and on how it was her fault I 'caught' cancer.

"As you know Gracie, I'm not a fan of drama so I just dialed everything back. I didn't tell Mom it was my younger sister who stole her car and crashed it and then walked home with a broken arm and pretended she hurt it when fell off her bike the next day.

"I didn't tell my other sister that I had a thing for her boyfriend, now her husband and we hooked up way before they did.

"I didn't tell my Dad that Mom, one night after my diagnosis when we got drunk together, Mom told me that she wasn't entirely sure that Dad was my biological father.

"Gracie, what purpose would it all serve if I rake all this stuff up? I'm sitting here in the Hospice because the cancer started eating up my body. But I'm not complaining about that. I'm complaining that no one will let me live while I can. My family cries when I laugh. I just want them to be able to laugh again when I'm gone.

"That's why I didn't phone you to come and see the family fireworks, because there weren't any. Why should I add to their tears?

"Although, I would love to see the look on my Sister's face when she found out that Dan and I were a thing before I dropped him like a hot potato. She always lords it over me that she's married and I'm not.

"I guess I won't be now, will I Gracie? But to the reason why I'm writing this letter-I have a two-part investigation for you and a confession. Here's the first part of the investigation.

"Remember how we talked about how Nurse Bartlett was stealing meds from the Hospice patients? Okay, she was even worse than that."

Gracie stopped reading and said to the cats who were curled up in her lap. "Petra wrote about Nurse Bartlett in the past tense. Did Petra do that because she knew Emma Bartlett was missing at the time, or because she knew Emma was dead? Curiouser and curiouser."

Gracie began reading again.

"Even though the staff at the Hospice are awesome, they are overworked and get a little task focused at times. They even forget that some of us can still get around and in general, our hearing is pretty good.

"I lurk around the Nurse's Station Gracie. They don't even notice me. I guess it's like you becoming self-employed as an investigator for something to keep your life interesting. I like to listen to the latest gossip because otherwise, it's pretty boring around here.

"About fourteen million times a day my Mom will ask me if I'm in pain (I'm not, because I'm pretty well medicated) and will ask me the same amount of times, if not more, if I would like something to eat. No. I'm not hungry. A person can only eat so much ice cream for breakfast.

"So I eavesdrop when my family isn't hovering around me. And I've heard the same complaints over and over again, from staff members, volunteers, and family members. They all are surprised at the amount of money the Hospice took from their accounts.

"For example, that weird smelling Mr. Payne was in this morning talking to the RN. He said that he thought he donated one hundred dollars, but his account was charged one thousand.

"Side point Gracie, he said that he was inspired by the life of one Gracie Noseworthy. Seriously, are you holding out on me? You can't be knocking boots with him! He smells like fish!

"Anyhow, he ended up saying that he didn't want to make waves, that he would just leave things as they were, but he wanted the RN to pass the information onto the financial office. He actually showed them his receipt for a charitable donation of one hundred dollars. He wasn't super mad, but he did insist that a new tax receipt be sent to him.

"Well Gracie, his experience is one of many. I've overheard so many people discuss this matter of bumped up donations and so many of them are confused but decide 'not to make waves.'

"And to a person, they all say something like, "I had that um, efficient Nurse run my card through. I would talk to her, but she's the one who's missing. I hope she's okay."

"Here's what I think. Not only did Nurse Emma rip off drugs from dying patients, but she also ripped off those people who donated to the Hospice. And I don't think anyone is reporting it.

"So that's what I would like you to investigate. I don't think the extra money all these people were charged went to the Hospice. I think it went into Nurse Emma's pocket!

"As payment I enclose one pair of pink runners. Ha! How's that for a contract and a payment?

"Now, on to the confession portion of this letter.

"I had to wait for several people to die. Me included. I know, it sounds weird, but you'll understand in a second.

"A group of us killed Nurse Emma."

Gracie blinked her eyes rapidly and informed her furless babies that her drink needed refreshing. She gently patted their bottoms

Gore in the *Garden*

to get them to slide off her lap. Frank gave her a sleepy cross-eyed stare, then jumped off and positioned himself in front of the treat cupboard. Zoey just curled up on the floor until Gracie opened the treat bag, then she was beside Frank like a shot.

After their treats, the cats settled themselves on the window seat while Gracie made herself a stronger rum and coke and looked at the pink running shoes with a sad little grin. Months ago, Gracie had asked Petra what size shoes she wore. In her usual irreverent manner, Petra had said, "Surprise me."

It was Petra who surprised Gracie. With her drink in hand, Gracie was ready to read the confession part of Petra's letter.

"You might know…" and here Petra wrote a list of five names of patients at the Hospice, "well, their life expectancy wasn't too much longer than mine. But you know, Doctors can get things wrong, so as a failsafe, I gave Mom this same list of names and asked her to mail you this package a month after we all were dead. I hope she does. Or maybe I should be writing, I hope she did."

"She did," said Gracie softly.

"We were in agony because of Nurse Emma. She not only withheld drugs, but she also withheld basic hygiene. She was a witch if there ever was one.

"It was kind of funny how we decided to kill her. It was happy hour and the six of us were sitting in the lounge drinking. No family or staff around and we were talking about which was worse, being in pain or being in wet diapers. I know, I know, Nurse Jasmine always reminds us that they are briefs, but they're adult diapers.

"Bob just said, 'let's kill her' and we all agreed. It was a simple as that Gracie.

"You should know by now, that for twenty-six years old, I'm pretty immature and I like me that way. But I did think about the morality of the matter. Did my morals go out the window because of seeing friends in pain? Or because I was going to die, and I wouldn't have to face the consequences? Or was it because I felt Nurse Emma Bartlett didn't deserve to live?

"I think it was all three things.

"So, how we were going to kill her was the next topic of discussion.

"We came up with a fitting death. Louise, who had a room furthest from the Nursing Station, would ask to be toileted at night when only Nurse Emma was around. Once Louise was up in the lift, she would say she changed her mind and asked to be put back to bed. But before Nurse Emma could lower the lift, Louise was going to shout, *I dropped my ring in the toilet! I'll pay you fifty bucks to get it for me.*

"Nurse Emma would probably agree to get the ring, but she would be angry to have to reach into the toilet. Gloves only go so high, you know. We wanted her to be beyond irritated when she died.

"Meantime, Bob would catch a ride with me because he was pretty weak and needed to save his strength. Yup, sitting on my lap while I cranked up the power on my wheelchair! We planned that Ann, Chester and Wally would already be in the room.

"Once Bob and I arrived, Chester would open the bathroom door and I'd wheel up and Bob would kick Nurse Emma in the butt. Wally would let the lift down and Louise would just sit on Nurse Emma.

"We didn't know how long it would take her to drown, so after Ann stole the keys, she would be the guard at the door in case the other nurse came back from her break earlier than usual.

"Well Gracie, our plan worked even better than we hoped.

"Nurse Emma was already angry when she came into Louise's room. When she saw Ann, Chester, and Wally there, she said "Oh, so you want an audience Louise? Far be it from me to stop you!"

Gore in the *Garden*

and she left the bathroom door wide open. Like I told you, she was a number one grade A witch!

"When Louise yelled out, 'I dropped my ring' etc., Nurse Emma negotiated for a hundred and fifty dollars. When Bob and I arrived, there was Nurse Emma bent over the toilet searching for the imaginary ring.

"Bob gave her a good boot and Wally was on the control button like lightening. The sling was a bit slow in lowering, so Bob kept kicking her.

"Once Louise was sitting on her, Ann had the keys and stood by the door. Chester felt a little left out, because he didn't have to open the bathroom door, so he searched Nurse Emma's pockets.

"Gracie, you would never believe what he found! Not only vials of hydromorphone, but several syringes. Chester took the initiative and injected her with all of whatever was in the needles.

"We decided to leave the vials in her pocket just in case anybody found her body. Bet you're wondering what we did with her body. I'll tell you in a minute.

"I've got pretty good upper body strength even yet, so I pulled Louise out of the sling in a kind of bear hug and Chester, Wally and even Bob, helped balance Louise while I rolled over to her bed and she kind of flung herself on it. Wally threw a blanket over her, because she was pretty much naked from the waist down, but Louise was fine with her lack of clothing.

"It's all bought and paid for boys!" she said. That Louise. What a card! Much later, she even rang for help and blamed Nurse Emma for leaving her there on the bed hours before. The next nurse was appropriately horrified.

"But back to the body and what we did with it. Ann had walked down to the utility room and unlocked it with Nurse Emma's keys and brought out one of those big green garbage bins and rolled it to Louise's room.

Shelley Dawn Siddall

"We used the sling to hoist Nurse Emma out of the toilet and dump her in the garbage bin. Then all of us, except Louise and Bob, took out the garbage. Yes Gracie, we used the keys to open the back door and rolled the bin out to be picked up by the sanitation department as part of their regular routine.

"That's my confession Gracie. I hope you don't think less of me; but even if you do, I won't care. I'll be dead.

"Now here's the second part of the investigation. Nurse Emma's body went missing, but I think I know what happened to it. After we killed her, we did get worried that the body would be found too quickly. I mean, the Huckleberry landfill isn't so huge that a body dumped from a garbage truck wouldn't be noticeable.

"So we would see one another and shrug and say, "What are they going to do to us? Give us a life sentence? We already have one." Did I feel remorse at what we had done? No. I kept getting the giggles. The Staff noticed and suggested that my pain meds were too strong, but they weren't going to do anything about it.

"Which was nice. I was finally enjoying life. By enjoying life, Gracie, I meant being able to sleep for at least four hours at a stretch before the pain woke me up.

"But enough of that. I don't know if I was curious or scared, but I decided to look in the garbage can the next night.

"It was empty.

"Here's something else you may not know Gracie, but Huckleberry does have a seedy underbelly. A guy we called 'Crackhead Billy' used to come by most nights and search the garbage bins for drugs even though he had been told that the Hospice isn't in the practice of throwing out drugs.

"Well, we throw out the occasional Nurse with drugs in her pocket, but that's not routine.

Gore in the *Garden*

"Security would find him sleeping in the back most mornings and run him off. Oddly enough, the night after we killed Nurse Emma, we haven't seen Crackhead Billy.

"I think he found Emma's body, found the vials of hydromorphone, used them and got higher than a kite. When he came down, he saw Emma's body and figured he killed her and then hid the body and then moved onto another town.

"In other news, the floor of the gazebo was undergoing some repairs at the same time. I think he hid the body there. The second part of the investigation then, is up to you. You have to decide if there is any good reason to find Nurse Emma's body.

"Is there actually someone out there who misses her?

"And is there any good reason to inform the families of six dead people that their loved ones were murderers?

"Does one outweigh the other?

"Gracie, I know this is a lot to take in, but from the short time I've known you, I think you can handle it. After all, you were the woman who joked with a double amputee about racing up a mountain. And then bought her a pair of pink runners.

"Did you see what I wrote on them?

Thanks for listening Gracie and I hope you are not too disgusted with me.

I'm not."

Petra.

***

"So what was written on the runners?" Ted asked. They were standing in the Gazebo in the front of the Hospice.

Gracie asked Ted to meet her there because she had a conundrum. She didn't tell Ted about the contents of the letter. It had disturbing information that she wasn't sure she should reveal as it was told to her in confidence. But Gracie told him about the pink runners.

"They had quotes written on their soles in surprisingly good penmanship. The right one says, "I was so sad that I had no shoes until I met a man who had no feet. So I said, "Got any shoes you're not using?"

Ted frowned. "That's terrible. What does the left one say?"

"Some people are anchored to this world by their feet, others by their fears."

Ted nodded. "Well that one's good. So, do you want to tell me about this foot person or is that part of your conundrum?"

Gracie changed the subject. "Look at these carnations. Such a beautiful red. And so durable. Just think, it was only two months ago this gazebo was ripped apart due in part to that, ahem driving *incident* with Trudy-Faye..."

Ted interrupted. "The so-called driving incident wherein her brakes failed at the time and never did again despite our rigorous testing of her brakes."

Gracie nodded. "And the subsequent discovery of rotten floorboards that needed replacing. Two months ago some idiot carpenter actually threw the rotten boards all over the flower bed and yet the carnations have thrived despite being in the middle of a construction zone!"

Ted bowed to Gracie's train of thought. He knew she was working things out.

"And speaking of things thriving, our relationship is doing quite well despite my flower fiasco!"

They both chuckled. Ted had decided to get a 'just because' gift for Gracie. He knew she liked peonies, so he bought her a beautiful blown glass sculpture that doubled as an ornate vase. As he walked up to her home, in a fit of inspiration, he cut one of her dark crimson peonies and placed it in the center of the gift.

Gore in the *Garden*

Gracie wasn't home, so he let himself in with his key, filled the vase with water and admired how the peony gracefully floated on the top. He snapped a photo then left the gift on the kitchen table.

When Gracie came home, her cats were having fun chasing ants. Ted wasn't a gardener and had tuned Gracie out when she told him about her solution to stop the ants from climbing up the stalks of her beautiful peonies.

She was not going to use poison bait, so instead she wrapped tape around the stalks, sticky side out, to catch the ants.

Apparently, it wasn't effective. As the peony blossom opened in the water, the ants came out and climbed out. Ted had shown the photo to Gracie to prove that the ants were hiding. She thought the whole thing was hilarious.

Gracie kissed Ted. "You were forgiven immediately."

Another longer embrace followed.

Suddenly Gracie pushed Ted away and announced, "She had a boyfriend!"

"Had?" Ted asked. "What is this had business? Was that kiss so bad I've been fired as a boyfriend?"

"No, I'm thinking about Nurse Emma Bartlett. She had a boyfriend. Do you think he misses her?"

"I think he misses the drugs she used to sell him." Ted pointed to Gracie. "And that's something the general public doesn't know at this point. I'd like to keep it that way."

Gracie started to look at her feet. She squinted her eyes to try and look between the floorboards in the gazebo.

"Pauline said she had no family to speak of. But what about the theft of thousands of dollars of donations?" Gracie rubbed her jaw while Ted's jaw dropped open. Gracie said slowly, "Was the boyfriend complicit in the defrauding scheme?"

"I don't know where you get your information from, my dear Gracie, but that information is not for public consumption either!"

Gracie reached over and picked a carnation and placed it behind her left ear.

"If we were in Hawaii, this would mean I'm off the market," she said.

Ted groaned. "If we were in Huckleberry, which wait a minute, we are, this would mean you are trying to distract me. Gracie, please tell me what you know about this missing nurse."

"You know this spring when we had a plethora of bodies in garden ponds?" she began.

"Oh good lord, don't tell me Nurse Emma is in a pond somewhere? And never use the word plethora again in the same sentence as bodies!"

Gracie was silent. She continued to weigh the repercussions of keeping the contents of the letter from Petra Kennedy secret against the harm it would do if the contents were revealed.

She stamped her foot several times. "Do you think this floor is as secure as it should be?"

Ted sighed. "I wish we could have just kept kissing, but you had to have a conundrum. In your oh so subtle way, I'm sure you're telling me Nurse Emma is buried in the gazebo."

Gracie whispered even though no one was around, "You might want to ask Crackhead Billy why he put her body there."

Ted put on his serious policeman face. "Just tell me this Gracie, is this letter a confession from Crackhead Billy that he killed Nurse Emma Bartlett?"

Gracie stared him in the eye and said honestly, "No, it is not a confession from Crackhead Billy. It is not even from Crackhead Billy, but the letter is full of what you might call hearsay."

Ted remained serious. "Yet, you have reason to believe that he put the body in the gazebo?"

"I do and I wish you could go ask him instead of grilling me."

Gore in the *Garden*

"And I wish you could say those words 'I do' under different circumstances, but neither of us are going to get our wishes granted. Crackhead Billy overdosed the same night Nurse Emma went missing."

Gracie was overjoyed. "Well that's good news! An open and shut case, I'd say."

She stamped her feet more forcefully and then started jumping. "Let's open this baby up and see what we can find!"

Crackhead Billy had indeed dragged Nurse Emma to the open pit in the gazebo and covered her up with a thin layer of dirt. As a former carpenter, Billy Gervais aka Crackhead Billy, still had the skill to nail some decking to the framework. When the regular carpenter arrived the next day, he saw that his job was partially completed and didn't question the reason. The regular carpenter just finished the job.

Gracie's stamping jarred the body. Her jumping jarred the skeleton even further. As it shifted a now rusted pin snapped from a nameplate which fell into the dirt.

Finally, Emma Bartlett was no longer falsely identified with the honorable profession of being a Nurse.

Shelley Dawn Siddall

Reap What You Sow?

Lila Jeffries was cold. The kind of cold that makes you hate everyone and everything. She piled on the blankets, but still her bones rattled.

She was filled with resentment and excuses. It was everybody's fault that she had to live this way. Her deadbeat husband that went and died on her decades ago and left her with a crippling mortgage and two brats.

She hadn't seen the boy or the girl in years. "Probably wouldn't recognize them even if they did come around," she muttered.

She could see her breath in the air. It was almost summer, and yet she had icicles hanging from every piece of furniture in her house. It was those damn microwaves. They went through everything and changed it. Even her brain. They put electricity into her brain.

And now they were trying to freeze her to death.

The Doctors didn't believe her.

Well she didn't care anymore. She was going to do get those microwaves if that was the last thing she did.

She turned up the heat.

Lila Jeffries did not have icicles in her house. What she had were bats in her belfry.

Gore in the Garden

She was crazy, but finally she was warm. She had cranked up the heat, put on all her clothes and lay down on the couch and piled on the blankets.

She could feel the heat seeping back into her bones and pushing those microwaves out.

Lila looked over at her plants, swaying with the current of warm air blasting from the furnace. She thought they were dancing.

They were so green, so vibrant. All the icicles had gone.

"You like the warmth, don't you my darlings?" she cooed. "Mommy is taking good care of her girls, isn't she?"

She had fed them that morning. Peanut butter and jelly sandwiches. For the smaller plants, she cut the sandwiches into quarters.

Some of her plants were a bit finicky, so she cut the crusts off.

She was a good momma to her girls.

Lila smiled. She heard the humming of the furnace and thought it was her darling plants singing to her.

"That's very nice girls," she said.

Lila Jeffries closed her eyes and died.

***

"They're going to be here at 11:30," Trudy-Faye told Gracie, "Are you going to be ready?"

It was the day of the garden tour and all of Huckleberry was coming if you were to believe Trudy-Faye Gervais.

Gracie didn't. Having been a regular tour attender in the past, she knew that maybe twenty people showed up for the first garden stop. Of that twenty, about five would get lost trying to find the next spectacular garden home, as Trudy-Faye had the advertisement read; another five would get bored and leave. But about ten would hang in there for the luncheon. So Gracie had prepared for twenty. She had many freezer containers on stand-by to package up the leftovers she was sure there would be.

Except for fudge. If there was any leftover it would all go home with Pauline, who even now, with breakfast barely out of the way, was eating her second piece.

"Girl, how do you stay so slim?" Trudy-Faye asked.

Pauline popped the rest of the maple fudge in her mouth and shrugged. "Don't know; good genes I'd say!"

Gracie laughed. "Too bad Dave wasn't here, or he would heartily agree!"

Trudy-Faye looked at Pauline who was wearing a pair of straight legged bedazzled denim. Trudy-Faye was confused as usual. Why would Dave be happy about her lineage? Cops were crazy. Just like the ones that showed up at her door about two months ago insisting she was next of kin to a local druggie called Crackhead Billy. Of course she wasn't.

Her son, William Lawrence Gervais, was overseas in Dubai doing carpentry work for some project in the oil industry. He wasn't the best communicator; he hadn't phoned or written in ages, but he was a good boy. Always had been despite what the teachers had said when he was growing up. It was amazing how the most elite schools could hire the stupidest teachers.

She checked her roster. A late entry was hand-written on the bottom of her sheet. Barry Frederickson and Barb Shire.

Oh the scandal! Barry wasn't even divorced yet from his murderous wife and Barb! Well, Barb had been under house arrest until recently. Still, they brought the group total up to twenty-five. The highest number in years.

Gracie made up two small bowls with each kind of soup for Trudy-Faye to sample.

Trudy-Faye had never eaten cold soup before; but if it was a thing the hoi polloi were doing, she'd give it a try.

Gore in the *Garden*

"This red soup is surprisingly delicious," she said after a tentative sip. "Is it hard to make?"

Gracie went over the easy recipe and explained that fresh lemon slices would be added just before it was served. Gracie knew that Trudy-Faye liked to be in control of everything. Something as simple as unexpected lemon slices on soup might cause her to flip out.

"If you heat this one up, it would be a lovely stew," Trudy-Faye said after she tasted the vichyssoise.

Pauline laughed, but Gracie just smiled.

Trudy-Faye continued to inspect the lay-out of the dining room until Gracie gently took her by the hand and led her to the front door.

"And we're done now. See you later," Gracie said kindly, but firmly as she dismissed the garden tour coordinator.

Pauline exploded. "How dare she tell you what to serve! It's your donation; your home. If I were you I would have decked her!" She quickly added, "But of course I really wouldn't because as a Huckleberry Police Officer, I maintain self-control and decorum at all times. And dignity; always dignity."

"One, two, three and..." Gracie paused and pointed to the front door.

Trudy-Faye burst in. "Cloth napkins! You are using cloth napkins?" she demanded.

With an absolute straight face, Gracie answered, "I was up all night trying to make them into swans, but I failed miserably."

Trudy-Faye walked over and patted her on the shoulder. "Just put them in napkin rings dear, and people will just have to live with them. At least you tried." She somehow was able to burst out of the front door as she left.

Pauline could not even grasp what had just happened. "Trudy-Faye is so bossy! How could you stay so calm? And you were so nice too."

"Oh, at the end of the morning, you may want to revise that statement."

Pauline knew Gracie had something up her sleeve. "Spill," she ordered.

Gracie walked over to the counter and picked up the advertisement for the garden tour. "You've never been on a garden tour before have you?" she asked Pauline.

Pauline shook her head. "I'm not paying five bucks for a dumb tour, no offense. I can see flowers for free as on my job I've driven to every corner of Huckleberry. Sometimes twice in one day."

"Good point Pauline, but people like to participate to get different ideas and inspiration for their own gardens Typically, you sign up, pay your five bucks and you're given a map to the private homes. The homeowner may give a little history behind their plants or point out interesting features. But in Huckleberry, we have a kind of tradition for our annual garden tour."

Gracie handed the tour list to her friend. "Read the first stop on the list."

Pauline gasped. "The Hospice? Where the team is digging up Emma Bartlett? Oh, this is too good. Trudy-Faye is going to flip her wig!"

Gracie poured them each another cup of coffee and smiled contently. "I may have purposely neglected to inform Trudy-Faye of the, ahem, additional festivities planned for today. So you see, I'm not really nice after all."

***

Gore in the *Garden*

He peeked in the window. All he could see were plants blocking the view inside. "Well I'm not breaking in," he said.

The owner of the home had not answered the door, so he decided to check out the back yard. It wasn't fenced. Just a dry patch of grass with an old, rusted swing set surrounded by cracked and crumbling concrete.

"I feel sorry for the kids who grew up here," he said. "What a sad life they must have had."

Conrad Jeffries had so distanced himself from his childhood memories, that he talked about himself and his sister Mary-Anne in the third person.

He had to see his Mother; it was time, but with his record, he wasn't even going to rattle a door handle and leave his prints behind.

Conrad went to a local coffee shop and considered his next move. He didn't want to involve the cops at this point. He would need them later to evict his Mother.

The cheery waiter interrupted.

"How's the coffee? New to town? Passing through or visiting?"

Conrad blurted out the truth. "I'm thinking about moving here."

"How wonderful! Look, I'll give you the local paper and a Danish on the house so you can really get to know Huckleberry. We have some beautiful old homes here. Of course, they're all fixer-uppers, but it will be something to do until you get a job. Or maybe you have a job? What do you do for a living?"

"I've recently been re-trained in accounting. I'm still quite a few courses away from being a CGA."

The waiter kept chatting despite his promise to get Conrad a Danish. "Are you looking for wirk or work? You know, internet work or nine to five?"

Conrad continued honestly, "I don't know, perhaps internet bookkeeping? Something I could do from home. I'm not very good with people in enclosed spaces."

The waiter looked around the cramped coffee shop and quickly decided to go get the pastry and newspaper and leave the scary looking man alone.

As Conrad looked through the paper he noticed a peculiar advertisement in the personal section. It read:

"Did you do something bad, but can't quite remember? Did your neighbor do something bad, and you want to get the goods on them? Contact Gracie Noseworthy Investigations at 555-2368. I sniff out trouble!"

***

Trudy-Faye was apoplectic. Yards and yards of yellow crime scene tape sectioned off most of the Hospice and no one was being allowed on the property except medical staff and families.

It was outrageous! No one had informed her that they would be digging up the gazebo looking for, of all things, a dead body!

She had demanded to speak to the Officer in Charge, and sure, Detective Sergeant Ted Bailey had walked up to her, but he had stopped her complaints before she had opened her mouth.

"I'm sorry Trudy-Faye; no one is allowed on the property. Your tour of this facility is cancelled."

And he walked away.

As Trudy-Faye stood there stewing, she realized she hadn't been this angry since two months ago when those cops played that horrid prank on her. Her son was in Dubai, not dead in the morgue!

Even her normally milquetoast husband was in on the gross morgue joke.

Gore in the *Garden*

"It's him. I saw him. They've matched his fingerprints and everything."

"No." Trudy-Faye refused to believe it. Just as she refused to believe William junior's teachers and many employers over the years. Just as she refused to listen to rumors about her precious son living in Munson not Dubai. Living in an apartment with a woman!

No. She had his letters that he sent every week. Well, not every week, because he was so busy. Every month or so, he would send a letter asking for money because the company kept screwing up his paycheck, what with the exchange rate and all.

Trudy-Faye had a busy life; she couldn't keep track of every little detail. That's what she told her husband when he asked her why the letters were mailed from Munson.

"Oh something about a buddy of his who works internationally but lives in Munson and a courier bag or something. I can't pay attention to every little detail for heaven's sake."

If Trudy-Faye had been paying attention, she would have realized that it had been over a year since she had received a letter asking for money. And it had been more than fifteen years since she had seen her son.

Right now, she was more concerned about a strange feeling of impotence. A scream was building inside her and she was frightened. She knew if she started to scream she wouldn't stop.

Just then, Barbara Shire came up to her. True love had changed Barb. She gave Trudy-Faye an uncharacteristic hug.

"You were so brilliant to put the Hospice as the first stop on the list! This is fascinating."

Trudy-Faye was numb. She looked at the pile of boards flung hither and yon, completely crushing the carnations.

The carnations probably wouldn't make it back from second assault against them.

Trudy-Faye looked forlornly at the taped off entrance and at the knot of staff and patients watching the deconstruction of the gazebo.

On a mound of dirt, the Director of the Hospice was talking to Detective Bailey and pointing to a huge piece of machinery.

"Look at the size of that crane! I heard they are just going to tear the whole gazebo down! The Detective is probably telling the Director that she will need to keep the facility locked down longer if the whole gazebo is going," Barry Frederickson said as he came up to where Barb and Trudy-Faye were standing.

"Oh this is going to be so interesting!" Barb continued to gush. "This is the same crane they used to pull my concrete planters out of my pond. It's amazing how precise they can be! They'll probably just cut the support posts and lift the whole top off."

A large truck stopped on the other side of the gazebo.

Other members of the garden tour group were gathering around Trudy-Faye, Barb, and Barry. They too, were offering a play by play commentary on the action.

"See, now the driver is going to ask where they want him to park so they can load gazebo on the flat deck."

"Look at that! They only have one guy with a reciprocating saw cutting through the posts. It's going to take forever!"

"They can't do anything until they get the body out."

"Did they get the body out yet?"

Barb Shire yelled over to Ted Bailey, "Did the meat wagon do a pick-up yet?"

True love may have changed Barb into a more affectionate person, but it certainly didn't refine her.

Anderson Payne, who had inched a little closer to Barb when she said 'pond', answered, "I came early and saw the Coroner's vehicle leaving; so yes, they have picked up the body."

Gore in the *Garden*

There was a collective groan in the tour group, but they continued to watch the events with fascination. There was even a round of applause when the top of the gazebo was lifted and placed on the flat deck truck.

Trudy-Faye was congratulated so many times for having the Hospice as the first stop on the tour, that she lost count. She also lost her urge to scream so that by the time the group arrived at Gracie's home, Trudy-Faye was in such a sunny mood that she ate a bowl of potato leek soup without heating it up.

The cats were not in a sunny mood. All through the meal they were yowling about the indignity of being locked up in the spare bedroom.

Gracie asked all her guests if they would mind if the cats were let out, and they all said it would be fine.

Zoey and Frank skittered across the hardwood floor and ran to the front door, where they each began a love affair with the footwear. Frank tried to stuff his whole body into a pair of boots while Zoey lay contently on a pair of loafers while she sniffed a pair of flats.

For those people who had never seen hairless cats, it was another worthy experience in a day of unique events. Some actually thought Gracie had released large rats from the room! Others fell in love with the warmth of their skin when the kitties decided to visit and deigned to be patted.

Anderson Payne, in particular, was converted. Zoey and Frank showed him such extra love that he got down on his hands and knees to talk to them, just as he did with his fish. Both felines head butted him several times to show their approval of this nice smelling man.

But when the phone rang, it broke the spell. The cats retreated to the spare bedroom, dug under the covers of the bed, and went to sleep.

"Is this Gracie Noseworthy? The investigator?" the husky voice asked.

"Yes, please hold for a minute."

Gracie thanked her guests for coming and asked them to sign the guest book and show themselves out.

"And, oh, please take some rhubarb and strawberries home with you! I have some bags filled at the front door. First come first served!"

She too retreated to the spare bedroom, grabbed a pen and paper, and returned to the call.

"Go ahead please."

"Hi. This is Conrad Jeffries. My Mom lives here. She's not answering her phone or her front door when I went over there today. I'm wondering if you could see why."

"Hello Conrad Jeffries. Could it be that she just wants some alone time and is ignoring you?"

Gracie heard a big sigh. "That's the problem in a nutshell," said Conrad sadly, "She told me this week she needed to be alone to fight a battle only she could fight."

"Yes?" Gracie prompted. She heard another big sigh.

"Mother told me the 'microwaves' were taking over and trying to freeze her to death. Every week it's something else. Last week, her plants were terribly sick, too sick for company. The week before the 'neighborhood hoodlums had stolen her car' and she had to file a police report. Mom has never driven in her life. She doesn't have a car. I'm trying to get her into a care home, but she isn't opening the door to anyone, let alone a Community Nurse to assess her. She distrusts any medical professional and for good reason. She's had quite a turbulent history with them."

"I'm so sorry Conrad and please call me Gracie. Have you asked the police to do a wellness check?"

Gore in the *Garden*

"I would, but I've had problems with the police in the past. I'm afraid they wouldn't take me seriously. Gracie, I think they would think I'm trying to kick my poor old Mom out of her home so I would have somewhere to live."

Gracie heard her company leaving. She also heard the embarrassment in Conrad Jeffries voice.

"Please Conrad, tell me the whole story so I can see if you should hire me and why you think the police won't believe you."

"I just got out of prison. Many years ago, with my Mom in and out of mental hospitals, my Sister Mary-Anne and I decided that living anywhere would be better than living at home."

"How young were you when you made that life decision? I take it your Dad was no longer in the picture?"

At the mention of the word Dad, both cats peered out from the covers. Gracie and Ted had fallen into the habit of referring to Ted as their Dad. They loved Ted and raced out of the room to look for him. Gracie ran out as well to make sure the front door was firmly shut.

It was.

Not finding Ted at the front door, the cats continued to search. They checked under each dining room chair and hopped up on the table to sniff around a flower arrangement just to make sure Ted hadn't fallen in. While Gracie continued to talk to Conrad, Frank was able to sneak up on the kitchen counter and stick his nose into the dishes that had been cleared from the table, but not washed. Not finding Ted, he jumped down and headed to the front door again and began checking Gracie's shoes in earnest. Zoey sat down, looked over her shoulder at Frank, pronounced him an idiot and began an extensive grooming session.

Other than therapy in prison, Conrad hadn't discussed his upbringing with anyone. He found it easy to talk to Gracie Noseworthy.

"Dad died when we were babies. Mary-Anne and I ran off when I was fourteen and she was sixteen. We had been in temporary foster homes in the past when Mom was in the hospital; but we ran away when she wasn't. She didn't seem to notice we were gone so nobody knew to look for us.

"I'm not blaming my Mother, it wasn't her fault, but it was too hard living in a war zone. Mom was always fighting some imaginary foe. Mary-Anne and I had big plans to go to the east coast, but we found living on the street not as glamourous as we thought. I started stealing radios, cd players and graduated to cars. I had a warm place to sleep, a full belly and a group of people I thought were my friends.

"Mary-Anne wasn't as lucky as me, she overdosed our second month out on our own."

He heard Gracie gasp.

"How tragic. At fourteen be all alone in the world. It must have been tough."

"It was but I made my choices, it was nobody's fault but my own. When I phoned Mom to tell her about Mary-Anne, she was too busy telling me about her new babies; apparently she bought a bunch of houseplants."

Gracie stood up, brushed imaginary lint off her slacks and asked, "Have you eaten?"

"I had a Danish here at the coffee shop."

"I'm going to pack you a lunch and come and pick you up. We are then going over to your Mom's house. Which shop are you at?"

***

"Hello, Lila Jeffries? It's me, Gracie Noseworthy!" Gracie shouted as she pounded on the front door.

The large man beside her whispered, "Do you know her?"

Gore in the *Garden*

Gracie shook her head. "No, I just figured a friendly greeting might encourage her to open the door."

Together they walked around the large house. Gracie unabashedly peered in as many windows as she could, but like Conrad, she found plants blocked her view.

"I'm afraid something is really wrong here, but I don't know what," she told Conrad. "Look at the moisture on the windows. She's got the heat up so high; I can feel it out here. I'm going to call the police. Don't worry Conrad, I have friends on the force."

When Dave and Ted arrived, Ted greeted Conrad Jeffries with a firm handshake and Gracie with a kiss on the side of the cheek.

Conrad smiled. "I see what you mean by friends on the force or is that the customary greeting in Huckleberry?"

"It most certainly is," said Dave as he puckered his lips towards Gracie.

"In your dreams, Romeo," Gracie said. "Mind you, if your bowling average improves, I'll drop Ted in a heartbeat!"

Ted rolled his eyes and then reviewed Conrad's identification and other documents.

"So you told your Parole Officer you were coming here? Good. In fact, Conrad, he contacted us a couple of days ago to let us know you were on your way. I like this open communication we have, let's keep it that way, okay?"

Conrad nodded and watched as Constable Dave picked the lock on the door.

The smell hit them as soon as they opened the door. Conrad was told to wait outside. In no time at all, Ted and Dave were outside again.

"We are sorry to tell you, we have found an older female, deceased. Do you feel able to make an identification?" Ted asked.

Conrad nodded and followed Ted and Dave inside the house.

"Yes. That's my Mom, Lila Jeffries," Conrad said quietly.

She was on the couch, almost buried under blankets. Her skin was stretched thin over her bones like parchment. She looked like she hadn't eaten in days.

"What is with these dried-up sandwiches?" Dave asked. He had turned the furnace off and had finished searching through the house for any other occupants, dead or alive. There was nothing living in the house.

Gracie had stepped into the foyer and watched Conrad as he slowly raised his eyes from his Mother and looked at the myriads of potted plants. Every plant was covered with a thick layer of dust.

Conrad looked closer at a plant.

"What the hell?" he yelled. He grabbed the nearest plant, barged by Gracie, and stormed outside.

Ted, Dave, and Gracie quickly followed.

Conrad ripped the plant out of its pot.

"It's fake. It's plastic."

He went back inside the house and brought more plants out.

He started ripping the plastic leaves off a plant.

"They're fake. They're all fake. Her damn plastic plants were more important than her daughter."

He crumbled into a heap and started sobbing.

***

It was several hours later. Gracie and Ted were talking quietly in Gracie's living room while Conrad snored in the spare bedroom.

"He'll be fine. The cats have given him their stamp of approval."

"Well, if Zoey and Frank approve, who am I as a Policer Officer to offer my opinion?" Ted grumbled.

"It's only until the house is cleared out. Apparently, Lila banked every pension check and every disability check she was ever sent.

Gore in the *Garden*

While she had her bills paid through the bank and had a meager amount of groceries delivered each month, she managed to save a sizeable sum. Julia down at the grocery store told me she mainly bought bread, and peanut butter and jelly. What was I saying?" Gracie was on her third rum and coke and was a little sleepy.

"Conrad now has the money to update the house and until its livable, he'll stay here, rent free. Now that I think about it, he has shown a real depth of forgiveness. Imagine, he has already made arrangements for a small service and a decent burial. That speaks to his character for sure."

Ted shrugged. "I guess it's okay if he lives here for a month or two."

He thought Gracie was asleep, but she piped up, "And speaking of depth, how far down was Emma Bartlett? Imagine, two dead bodies in one day."

"Not far." Ted sipped his drink. "And what a difference in mothers. Trudy-Faye sent her son to get the best education money could buy, and Lila Jeffries didn't even know her son was gone or even care that her daughter died."

Gracie had filled Ted in on what Conrad had told her about his family life.

Ted continued, "So one boy has all the material advantages in life you could ask for and the other has none. Both end up in the gutter, but the one with the roughest start in life was able to eventually turn his life around."

"With the help of many taxpayers financing his stay in one of our more gated communities," Gracie added. "But what is this about Trudy-Faye's Son? Hasn't he been working in Dubai for years?"

"As usual, I've told you too much. I may as well continue. Firstly, Mr. William Lawrence Gervais has never held a passport in his life."

Gracie sat up and blinked her eyes repeatedly.

"Secondly, you knew him as Crackhead Billy. He overdosed the night he dragged Emma Bartlett's body into the gazebo. We don't know if he killed her or someone else did, but we do know that Trudy-Faye refuses to believe he is dead. She thinks he's in Dubai."

Gracie was processing this information by continuing to blink her eyes rapidly.

"How can a mother be so out of touch with her children?" she asked.

Ted thought about this for a bit. "We really can't blame Lila Jeffries; she had a long history of mental illness. Yes, she abandoned her children in every way imaginable, but when it comes down to it, she intentionally did nothing wrong. Trudy-Faye, on the other hand…"

"Trudy-Faye is a bully. She bullied William Senior into marrying her when she was pregnant by someone else."

Ted raised his bushy eyebrows at this.

"Oh Ted, the things we women talk about at our little wine parties. Anyhow, she had the baby and then got bored with it. Excuse me, not it, but with William Junior. She wanted him to be presentable, seen but not heard. And it seems to me she was on every committee ever. Anything to keep her name in the limelight so she could grow her real estate business. She was just too busy for a child. She figured she would just hire the right Nanny, send the child to the right schools and everything would turn out right. If anyone abandoned their child emotionally, it was Trudy-Faye."

"Comparisons," Ted mused. "Trudy-Faye treated her child like a potted plant whereas Lila Jeffries thought her potted plants were her children."

Gracie settled back down with her drink. "There's that old adage, you reap what you sow. But is Trudy-Faye really reaping what she's sown? She ignored her child most of his life and she's still doing it. His death hasn't touched her."

"It will."

"And let's look at Lila Jeffries. Is she really worthy of a Son who not only checked up on her by phone every week, for the three years he was in prison but who now gives her a decent burial? You know Ted, he's already paid for everything with the small amount of money he earned working in prison. He won't get any inheritance for weeks. Is Lila really reaping what she's sown?"

"I think we have to look at this in reverse. Is Conrad really reaping what he has sown? He's worked hard to turn his life around. He worked hard to establish a relationship with his Mom despite her fog of mental illness. He came all the way out here as soon as he could to place her in a care home where she would be well looked after. Is he reaping what he's sown? I say yes. Despite his meltdown today, he's finally found peace. I mean, Gracie, listen to that man snore!"

On cue, Gracie started in with her own imitation of a chain saw.

She dreamed about planting seeds that grew into three big cabbages. She gently parted the leaves and found a beautiful baby in each cabbage. Somehow she carried all three babies close to her while she and Ted looked for a place to live. They were suddenly in a shopping Mall searching for a home among the stores. Ted found an empty store and they moved in. The cats were there now, and they were hungry, and the children were hungry. Everybody was crying.

Gracie told Ted, "I'm never leaving my children. Go out and bring back some bottles for the babies."

Ted chuckled as Gracie continued to talk in her sleep as they sat snuggled on the couch in her home.

"Go to the food court. If they won't give you anything, just shoot them and steal it."

Ted felt a little teary. It was a shame Gracie never had any children. She would have made one hell of a fine mom.

Gracie then added, "And you gotta teach the kids how to shoot people too."

Maybe not, thought Ted.

Mr. Pitre, Pickled And Potted In The Garden

"Eighty-sixsh bottles of beer on the wall, eighty-sixsh bottles on the wall, one fell off and..."

The singer stopped bellowing the old drinking song and began muttering.

"Now what a waste of alcohol. No thatsh not it. Where was I?"

Julia Smith opened her window and sang, "Fifteen. Fifteen bottles of beer on the wall."

The singer started his drunken serenade again. "Fifteen bottles of beer on the wall, fifteen bottles of beer!"

Julia slammed the window shut again. It was Friday night and Mr. Pitre was in especially fine form and, as per his routine, would be all weekend.

It was times like these that she really wished her husband was still around. He had disappeared a few months ago. The popular opinion was that he took off with that chick at the tanning salon, but Julia was pretty sure he hadn't.

If Brett was still around, he would have marched out there and yelled at Mr. Pitre as he had done in the past.

Actually, it didn't really make a difference if anyone yelled at Mr. Pitre. He'd simply smile and agree to stop singing and hold out whatever he was drinking for the irate neighbor to sample. And then invite the neighbor to join him in song. And he would sing even louder than before.

But Brett trying to get their neighbor to simmer down, made Julia feel better. With him gone, she was too frightened to yell at anyone, because they could get angry, and she had no one to protect her.

The young woman went back to what she was doing, finding her center. She wanted to be a 'go with the flow' kind of person and read that to do this she must 'find her center', but every time she tried to look inside herself, she didn't find much.

She rolled up her yoga mat and stashed it behind the couch. Now, on to her real passion; gardening!

Thankfully, Mr. Pitre had passed out around the emptying of the fifth bottle of beer from the wall so Julia dead-headed her marigolds in peace. It gave her so much joy to look at her new garden beds.

She had read about such a thing in an article on-line, but Brett had always said no to her ideas. A week after he disappeared it occurred to her that she could do whatever she wanted!

First, she went out and bought white sheets with a sateen stripe and put them on the bed. Without Brett and his dirty feet, the sheets stayed pristine!

Then she got all of her stuffed animals out of the suitcase Brett told her to put them in. She placed her doggies and bears and stuffed hearts all over her bed and took several photos and posted them on her social media account. She felt like she was sleeping in a penthouse suite in some fancy hotel.

Gore in the *Garden*

And that's what she did next. Julia had woken up one morning and decided she wanted to stay in a hotel. So she did. And she ordered sushi to boot!

Because of that stay, Julia would carefully fold the ends of her toilet paper to make it look like a maid had just cleaned her bathroom. She would always giggle after she did this and say aloud, "I must leave a tip for the maid; she always does such a fine job!"

Julia also realized she could now buy home and garden magazines to leave around the house, so she went to the thrift store and bought several dozen. The garden projects described inside the magazine pages were well within her financial reach and she did as many of them as she could fit in her yard.

Julia was nailing brightly colored gumboots to her fence when the garden bed project re-surfaced in her mind. She quickly filled up the gumboots with dirt, planted petunias and watered them, then hopped in Brett's truck.

Brett had disappeared without his truck. That's why she figured he was dead. He might leave Julia, but never his truck. And if he was somewhere hiding and watching her, well, he would pitch a fit if he saw her driving his truck. So, she was pretty sure he was dead.

As for the tanning salon woman? Julia had seen her working at another store over in Munson. The woman was just locking up the store when a man in a minivan pulled up. Julia could see a toddler in a car seat when the woman got in the vehicle. They looked like a nice little family.

Brett was not the man driving. He would not be caught dead in a minivan! Wouldn't it be funny though, if Brett was dead and the murderer transported him in a minivan?

Julia was thinking about all this when she drove to the landfill to look for metal bedposts. She found four of them, loaded them up and planted them that night.

They looked a bit funny at first, too close together, so she went in the house, found a tape measure, and measured the length of her bed and adjusted the bedposts. They still looked like they were going to fall over at any minute. It was a big day, so Julia cleaned up and went to bed, happy at the progress she was able to make. In the morning, the bedposts had sunk deeper into the dirt and now were straight and plum. They looked fantastic.

Even though she had plenty of money, she decided to go with marigolds. They were cheap, but so gorgeous! She planted one of her garden beds with densely packed yellow flowers while the other had the orange kind with red centers.

Of course, stuffy old Trudy-Faye Gervais had complained to other people, but Julia didn't care.

Even Mr. Pitre loved her flowers. And now that the bedposts were even more rusted, it all looked so beautiful. Julia was in heaven, except for one little thing.

Mr. Pitre's singing. It wasn't that he was drunk and loud; it was that he was out of tune. Completely tone deaf.

Julia had perfect pitch. It was what Brett noticed about her at the karaoke bar. Well, that and her legs. He always told her that her legs almost balanced out her face. He used to say, "Looks like you fell out of an ugly tree and hit every branch on the way down."

Julia sat and continued to dead head the flowers. She even loved putting the withered flowers in the basket as she worked in the cool night air. Somehow it made her feel pretty.

She was really doing some deep thinking tonight. She felt much better about herself now that Brett was gone. When they were together, she used to ask herself over and over again if Brett meant those things he said. Was Brett just joking or was he really mean?

Julia now knew that Brett was mean.

***

Gore in the *Garden*

Mr. Pitre woke up the next morning with another killer hangover. It was odd, he thought, that his hangovers were always worse on the weekend. Probably get a crick in my neck from sleeping on the couch and it cuts off the blood flow to my brain and gives me a headache, he reasoned.

He sat up and massaged his neck.

"Oh look who has finally decided to grace us with his presence!"

"Mrs. Pitre, why don't you go and take a long walk off a short pier," he retorted.

"Oh aren't we the funny one this morning. What time did you get in last night?" his wife said.

"As if you care!"

"Your nephew called. He wanted to know if you were still going fishing with him this weekend."

"Well, what did you say woman?"

"What could I say? You weren't here. That was the first I ever heard of any fishing trip. If you were home you could have answered the phone yourself."

Mr. Pitre was angry. "You're the one who 'repossessed' my phone! How the hell can I answer the phone if I don't have one!"

"You're the one who racked up hundreds of dollars drunk dialing your buddies all over tarnation! I tried shutting off the cellular data when you went out, but you still broke the bank account with your phone bill!"

"Heah, Evelyn, my name's Cliff. Why don't you drop over some time?"

Mrs. Pitre gave a long-suffering sigh from the kitchen. "You want coffee or not? Your mug is here. I'm not serving it."

Mr. Pitre drank his coffee at the kitchen island and looked out the window at Julia Smith's house. She was in her kitchen doing the dishes.

"Is it just me, or is she looking better and better every day?" he asked his wife.

Mrs. Pitre slammed down her coffee cup. "Don't even think about it Leon!" she said tersely.

"Oh God, Evelyn, she's probably a quarter of my age. No, I think since that no-good husband of hers disappeared, she's much better off. She seems happier too."

"Well truth be told; she was always a pretty little thing. Her husband was the one who was putting her down all the time. The things he would say to her!"

"I know," said Leon Pitre, "I was out in the yard one time…"

Evelyn smirked. "Passed out in the yard is more like it."

"You and I trade insults, but Brett was just plain mean. He told her she was uglier than a sack of…"

"Oh don't say it! I do not need that image in my head first thing in the morning!"

Leon started chuckling and looked at his wife and said, "You left the door wide open woman."

Despite herself, she started chuckling too. "Go ahead, say it."

He pointed to her and said with disgust, "And I do not need that image in my face first thing in the morning!"

***

"Yes," said Julia, as she was drying her dishes, "Mr. Pitre may be nice, but he is so annoying when he sings."

Julia had started talking to herself on a regular basis since Brett disappeared. She supposed she could get a pet, because she had read that talking to a pet was very therapeutic, but she didn't think she had the stomach to clean up after an animal.

She stopped and thought hard.

"I don't think I could kill him, could I?"

Gore in the *Garden*

Julia stooped down and looked under the sink. Brett had rat poison under there. They never had any rats, but Brett said better safe than sorry, so just before he disappeared, he bought a great big box. It wasn't even open.

"I could put some in a bottle of whisky and give it to Mr. Pitre to drink; but then, what if he got sick?"

Julia almost keeled over thinking about it.

"No, he'll just have to live, and I'll just have to get ear plugs."

In a rare moment of insight it occurred to Julia if anyone had heard the conversation she just had with herself, they might seriously question her sanity. Perhaps she should get herself a dog.

Julia spent a delightful morning watching funny dog videos. She really didn't have anywhere to go; her trust fund made sure that she would never have to work, plus Mr. Pitre in his more sober times had installed underground irrigation for her. She had carefully read the manual and set up a watering schedule for each garden zone. She set the start time for two o'clock in the morning as this was the most efficient use of water in the summer.

Or so she had read. That meant that her precious garden was already well-watered, and she could just sit and do nothing if she wanted to.

About one o'clock a very unfamiliar feeling began to overtake Julia. She was bored. She did not have a new project planned and was feeling a little deflated.

When Mrs. Pitre came over at one thirty with a pineapple upside down cake, Julia was thrilled beyond belief. It was just like in the magazines! A neighbor coming over with a cake and staying for coffee.

Oh and the things they talked about! Haircuts and dresses and nail polish! And, of course, gardening.

Mrs. Pitre told Julia how wonderful Julia's garden beds looked and that her back yard was divine.

"You know, when you planted rhubarb on top of those pillars, well I didn't quite know what to expect," Mrs. Pitre said, "but it's turned out so interesting. What you do need now is a fountain!"

Julia's eyes opened wide. She had several bird baths, but a fountain! Now that would be something.

"And you should put it right front and center, so everybody passing by your house will see it and…" Mrs. Pitre seemed a little loss for words. She had a sip of coffee. "And enjoy it's splendor!" she finished.

Julia was not the same Julia of a few months ago. Now she at least tried to guess how things worked.

"I could divert the water supply from the main drip tubing, just change out a fixture and connect it to the pump for the fountain."

"Well, I don't know if that would work dear," Evelyn Pitre said, "But I'm sure the folks down at the hardware store will help you. They have a nice girl down there; Marcia I think her name is and she is so helpful."

Mrs. Pitre leaned forward and confided, "Well, Mr. Pitre doesn't like her, I don't know why. He even avoids looking at her, but she's clever, that Marcia. She always tries to catch his eye and when she does, he gets so uncomfortable. Marcia and I just giggle and giggle!"

Something fell into place in Julia's brain.

"Oh no, she's not at the hardware store anymore. Didn't you see that article in the paper ages ago? She died in a pond accident."

The two women gossiped on about the fate of Marcia and the urgency of Julia's new fountain project.

"Oh, I think you should get started right away," urged Mrs. Pitre, "You could go ahead and dig the hole this afternoon!"

Julia was doing a search on the internet.

"Oh it's a closed system. I can't use the irrigation; in fact, that would be the absolute wrong thing to do. Also, who would want a fountain to only run at night? You're right, Mrs. Pitre, I better ask someone who knows how to do this!"

"But you can dig the hole this afternoon dear. Just do it right out front of your house, where everyone can see," Mrs. Pitre continued to harp on the subject. "And of course, you will be able to see it from your front room window! It will be magnificent!"

Julia nodded. She was still a bit unsure about the fountain in the front of the house. She kind of wanted it in the back, so she could sit out on her little deck in the morning and watch the water. But, she reasoned, she could go ahead and dig the hole and if she changed her mind, she could fill it back in.

"Mr. Pitre has a spade you could use. Do you want me to bring it over?"

***

"She actually brought the spade over to your house?" Gracie asked Julia.

They were sitting in Gracie's comfortable living room. Each had a cat curled up on their lap and a cup of jasmine tea on a side table.

Over on the kitchen table was a check and a carefully cut out newspaper clipping that read:

"Did you do something bad, but can't quite remember? Did your neighbor do something bad, and you want to get the goods on them? Contact Gracie Noseworthy Investigations at 555-2368. I sniff out trouble!"

The check Julia had written Gracie was unfiled. Gracie wasn't sure there was a case.

"Yes. Right after she left, she was back with it. She waited until I went out and started digging. It was hard work, let me tell you." Julia smiled and patted Zoey. The cat sensed that this was one of the gentlest beings in the universe and stretched and yawned happily.

Julia continued. "When she went in the house I kept digging, but I guess my mind was working too because suddenly I thought of Mr. Pitre. He'd be coming home drunk. He always walks home from the bar and cuts right across my front lawn. I don't mind, of course, but I realized that he would trip in the hole."

"Well that doesn't sound all that terrible," Gracie said, "What makes you think Mrs. Pitre was trying to kill Mr. Pitre?"

Julia looked off in the distance. "You know that feeling you get when someone is watching you? I just knew Mrs. Pitre was watching me so I kept digging. The more I dug, the more I wanted to tell her to go jump in the lake, I want my fountain in the back yard!"

Quite unlike other clients, Gracie had no desire to push Julia to get to the meat of her story. Gracie loved having this delightful young lady at her house. She had such an innocence about her and such a beautiful speaking voice.

"And did you tell her to jump in the lake?" Gracie asked.

"I didn't have the courage. No sooner had I finished digging a fairly wide and deep hole for the fountain reservoir, Mrs. Pitre came over and said she would help me chose the right kind of rocks." Julia sipped more tea. "You know Gracie, I did see a picture of this on the internet. You pile up the rocks like a tower and the tubing is hidden behind and the water just trickles down the rocks. It did look lovely."

"I imagine it did."

"So Mrs. Pitre went over to the dry river bed I built and started taking rocks from it and piling them on one side of the hole. In my mind, I saw Mr. Pitre stumbling home, tripping and then smashing his head on the rocks. I was nearly sick thinking about it."

Gracie narrowed her eyes at this last part of Julia's story.

"Now we're cooking with gas!" Gracie said. "Did you say anything to Mrs. Pitre about your concerns?"

Julia nodded sadly. "I did. She just laughed and said, well it's a good thing I've got a lot of life insurance out on him."

Gracie was alert now. "Did Mr. Pitre fall in the pit?"

"Oh no! I watched for him and walked him home. Today I went and bought a bunch of solar garden lights and put them all around the rocks and the hole. I decided to build a fountain there after all, but I am determined to build one in the back as well!"

Gracie thought for a bit. "Julia, it certainly sounds very suspicious, and you absolutely did the right thing with the solar lights and meeting Mr. Pitre. I'd like you to write this all down, while it's still fresh in your mind and sign it and I'll keep it in a file. If anything happens to Mr. Pitre in the future, I can bring your suspicions to the police."

Julia frowned. "Can't we do anything else?"

Gracie walked over to the table and picked up the check.

"I'd like to earn this check," she said, "And this is how. For the next few weeks, I will happen to bump into Mrs. Pitre wherever she goes and start discussing preventable accidents at home."

"But won't that give her even more ideas on how to murder Mr. Pitre?"

Gracie held up her index finger. "I'll also mention somewhat true-life stories of the aftermath of these accidents. The long convalescence at home and the strain on family members as they have to be at the beck and call at the person recovering from a fractured hip, or twisted ankle or whatever."

Julia got it. "So then Mrs. Pitre will think twice about trying to kill Mr. Pitre. She could just end up hurting him and then she would have him at home with her all the time!"

"Exactly!"

Julia left Gracie's home feeling lighter than air. She was so relieved that nice Mr. Pitre was safe. Oh yes, he still sang terribly out of tune, but he also was looking out for her. The least she could do was look out for him.

When she walked him home last night, she wanted to thank him again for all the irrigation work he had done for her. She knew what she wanted to say, but what came out of her mouth was, "Thank you for all the work you did underground!"

He chuckled and stopped walking. Julia tugged on him a bit, but he stayed rooted in place.

"Oh so you figured it out did you? That husband of yours, he wasssh a rotter! We got drunk one night and he told me he was gonna poison you with rat poison and inherit all your money. So I jes killed him. Yup. I bashed him over the head with my spade and buried him in your back yard. When you started getting into gardening, I dug him up and put him in your flower beds. I mixed up some quick set concrete, layered it on him, and sunk your bedposts back in. Then I put a whole pile of dirt over the concrete. I mounded it up like somebody was under the covers. And they were!"

Julia took this revelation calmly. *That's why the bedposts looked like they had been moved and were firmly embedded in the ground.*

Mr. Pitre had started to chuckle again. "Flower beds! That's hilarious. I love those things."

He started walking again and Julia stayed with him and helped him use his key to open his front door. She then walked home and looked fondly at her marigolds where Brett would be sleeping forever.

That was last night. This afternoon, Julia didn't tell Gracie Noseworthy any part of the discussion with Mr. Pitre. Mrs. Pitre trying to kill Mr. Pitre had nothing to do with Mr. Pitre killing Brett.

Gore in the *Garden*

Besides, Julia already figured Brett was dead, so she just filed the information away and forgot about it.

The definitely widowed Mrs. Smith returned home excited to start on her new projects. She was going to watch some videos on how to build fountains and then make a list of all the supplies she would need.

But first, she was going to sit by her marigolds and tell Brett just what she thought of him.

Shelley Dawn Siddall

The Garden Rake or Lettuce Alone!

Lothario. Rake.
Oh they had names for him over the years.
Lounge lizard, Ladykiller, Casanova, Snake. That last one bugged him.
He wasn't a snake. He just loved the ladies and they loved him. Sure, they were sometimes just a little bit older than him. Okay, maybe two sometimes three decades older, but heah, love was love. It knows no age.
That what he always emphasized. He had said those exact words not more than ten minutes ago to his current paramour, Hazel Froment. And he really, truly did love Hazel. It's just that he loved her money more.
He had just enough of a nest egg for wining and dining Hazel for two weeks. They went to the finest restaurants and ordered the finest wines.
Of course he had to look the part. Shane Mitchell knew the value of a custom-made suit. No off the rack suits for him, no sir! He had told Hazel he was 'just going to freshen up', but in reality, he wanted to look at himself in the mirror.

Gore in the *Garden*

At fifty-five, he still had it. Thick black hair, just long enough to say, 'bad boy' but not too long so that it said 'dandy'. Luxurious mustache and neatly trimmed goatee, a flat stomach, and beautifully manicured nails.

And his height. At six foot four, he really stood out in the crowd. For this engagement, as Shane liked to view his latest conquest, he had chosen to wear strikingly blue contacts. No wonder everyone in the restaurant turned to watch him as he walked back to the table. He was, quite frankly, dashing.

Shane had been dating Hazel for two weeks. She had been a tough nut to crack. He figured it was because she was a lot closer to his age; she was sixty-seven. They finally were entering the honeymoon phase, as Shane preferred to think about it. This was the time to strike.

He slid in beside her and accidentally on purpose jostled her arm, the one holding the wine glass.

"Darling, look what I've done! We must rush you back home and get you out of those wet things."

Hazel was appalled. She had gussied herself up, had her hair done and got this beautiful gown out of mothballs for tonight's date.

"Do you think club soda will take this stain out?" she asked while attempting to pat herself dry with her napkin.

"You go out to the car my darling," Shane said, "and I'll settle up the bill. Be with you in a jiffy! Hurry my darling, run!"

Shane approached the Manager as Hazel made a beeline to the car without thinking what the hurry might have been as she still had to wait for Shane to get in and drive,.

"Did you see my date run out of here?" Shane said snippily.

"Yes Sir, is there an issue?"

"Is there an issue? Is there an issue? I'll say. She took one sip of that subpar red wine and spit it out." Shane tapped the manager on the chest and said confidentially, "Not the most cultured woman I've dated, but she was right about the wine. It was atrocious!" Shane waited for the manager to make amends by comping their meal.

"But Sir, you have been drinking the wine all evening with your steak Neptune."

Damn, Shane thought, the disadvantages of a small town; on a Friday night the so-called fanciest restaurant barely had any customers. The manager could easily keep an eye on the patrons. This guy even knew what they were eating. Oh well, maybe he could get a discount.

"Perhaps you and your Mother would enjoy a coupon for a free dessert with the purchase of an entrée on your next visit?"

Shane pursed his lips and waved away the offered coupon. He reluctantly paid the full amount of their meal; only slightly mollified that the manager had called Hazel his Mother. At least, his good looks were holding up; the man thought there was at least twenty years between them instead of twelve.

"We won't be visiting your establishment again," Shane said as a parting shot.

"I shouldn't think so," agreed the Manager, "You've been here four times already this week. If you haven't got the fish on the hook by now, I'd just give up."

"You look all red in the face Shane, what's going on?" Hazel asked when he got in the car.

"Just angry at myself for ruining a perfectly good evening. But no worries, we can sit and cuddle at your place."

Hazel put her hand on his arm. "Shane don't be so hard on yourself. We'll work on getting this stain out of my dress and then we'll see where the evening takes us."

I've got her now, Shane thought. Oh no, he wasn't expecting marriage or sex for that matter. It's just that when these old dolls get all googly eyed around him, he could ask them for the moon, and they would give it to him. The last old biddy he had 'dated' parted with a check for over twenty thousand dollars. Not bad for two weeks work. He didn't even make up a good excuse. He just said, "I need money, Gertie, can you give me some?"

Fortunately, Shane had cashed the check the day before she popped off permanently. Her family was still trying to get the money back, but Shane was long gone from that town. Just like he'd pack his bags tonight and high tail it out of town.

He figured Hazel was good for at least twenty thousand. Shane hummed a tune while he drove and suddenly Hazel started singing along:

"Beautiful dreamer, wake unto me, Starlight and dew drops are waiting for thee; Sounds of the rude world heard in the day, Lull'd by the moonlight, have all pass'd away."

Again, she placed her hand on his arm and stared up into his face with a serene smile. Shane noticed that her fingers clasping his arm were pretty boney. Her rings will probably slip right off, he thought. Maybe I should avoid asking for a check and just take the rings? Nah, he thought, I'll go for both.

Hazel's house was like a beautiful but overstuffed recliner. It was very comfortably filled with antiques but also newer sculptures that could quickly be converted to cold hard cash. If Shane was a younger man, he might have gone for a more long-term relationship, because obviously Hazel had money, but with his history, he didn't think it was wise to stay in one place for too long.

He ran his finger along the top of what he was sure was a genuine Duncan Phyfe card table of solid mahogany. Shame, he thought.

But he wasn't that pool boy anymore. In the olden days, he had married a few cougars and when they got tired of him, they paid him to go away. No problem. But as he aged, arthritis was setting in along with a vague feeling he couldn't quite pin down. As he travelled from town to town or city to city, he found himself looking at gabled houses on maple lined streets.

He wished he could get a handle on this unsettled feeling. But enough wool gathering, on to the task at hand.

"Well I got the stain out! That club soda did the trick, but I'll still send my dress out to the dry cleaners. They're so expensive, aren't they, but worth every penny."

Hazel was not wearing a silk dressing gown as Shane had imagined she would be. She had on a jean jacket, blouse, and jeans. Plus she was wearing sneakers.

Hazel did not look like the frail little old lady Shane had been wining and dining the past two weeks. She looked determined.

Even her voice sounded different when she told him to sit down.

Shane sat down then did what he could to ease the tension. He made a little joke. "Going on a hike?"

Hazel laughed. Not a cute old lady giggle that Shane had heard before, but a braying belly laugh.

"Two weeks ago, I was ready to tell you to take a hike, Shane old boy!"

Shane blanched.

Hazel opened a drawer on a side table and pulled out a newspaper clipping and threw it at Shane.

"Read this and then tell me what you think I did."

He read:

"Did you do something bad, but can't quite remember? Did your neighbor do something bad, and you want to get the goods on them? Contact Gracie Noseworthy Investigations at 555-2368. I sniff out trouble!"

Shane was uncharacteristically at a loss for words. He shrugged and shook his head.

"I had my friend Gracie check you out! We go way back; do you know we started at Sears together?"

Shane's throat was dry. He managed to say, "I didn't know that."

Hazel laughed. "Course, I was much older than her, but recently widowed and bored." Hazel leaned forward and patted Shane's knee. "I get bored easily," she said.

"Oh yes?" croaked Shane. He really wished he had drunk a lot more of that wine at dinner.

"I found out you have a nasty habit of screwing little old ladies out of their money."

Her hand grabbed his knee in a death grip.

"Don't you even think of running away! You are going to sit here and listen to me. Picking me up at Bingo was pretty novel and very flattering. But I wasn't born yesterday. Many a gold-digger has come around trying to win my hand in marriage when what they really want is the millions belonging to the sole owner of the Froment Hotel chain.

"So I talked to my staff down at the Hotel and they told me you had been sniffing around earlier in the day, asking all sorts of questions about dear Mrs. Froment, and what was her schedule like these days? I phoned Gracie up and she did some quick searching; she may have used some facial recognition software I have access to because of my friends in the FBI. Do you know that my dear departed Mr. Froment assisted in several stings for the FBI? No matter.

"Gracie delivered a rather detailed file to me within a matter hours. You have left quite a list of broken hearts behind you, along with quite a few empty pocketbooks. Now, I knew all this before we even went on our first date. So why do you think I went ahead with it?"

Shane was, among other things, a quick study.

"You were bored."

Hazel's braying laughter rang out. "Right on, Shane! It's an affliction I had, even before I was obscenely wealthy. You were hilarious! All those smarmy words and so glib at the drop of a hat! I had such fun acting like a wide-eyed ingenue!"

Hazel put her hands under her chin and batted her eyes and smiled, "Oh Shane, how sweet of you to invite me for dinner! Oh Shane, how handsome you look in your suit. And your eyes, your eyes are incredible Shane; I could just get lost in them." Then she giggled a high silly giggle.

Shane's teeth were clenched but he attempted a smile. He was not in control and it was a very uncomfortable feeling. Her acting these past two weeks was hilarious, but only to Hazel. Not to Shane.

"Tell me Shane, did you try to get the restaurant to compensate you for the meal by saying the waiter spilled wine on me?" Hazel asked with a grin.

"Something like that." Shane was afraid to speak. Hazel, in the course of the evening, had turned into a terrifying interrogator who definitely had his number. He was afraid she also was recording this conversation, so he wasn't going to admit to anything.

"Oh don't worry Shane; I'm not recording us."

Great, Shane thought, I would try to swindle a mind reader. This is not going to end well.

"So Shane, I have a proposition for you. It's simple. I want to hear all about your life including your sordid life of crime. I've read every true crime book in the library, but to actually have a firsthand account would be marvelous. In return, you live rent free in my

Gore in the *Garden*

carriage house but during this time you will put your con man activities aside. Thoughts?"

"I do have one or two pressing matters that may interfere with your plan."

Hazel nodded. "Oh, you mean the twenty grand the estate of Gertie Hansen is trying to get you to return. Well, I've settled that for you as a token of my appreciation. I had so much fun!"

"Any other conditions before I take up residency?" Shane asked.

"Nope. We'll meet from, say three to five each afternoon and you'll tell me an event in your life. You'll receive a small, shall we say, stipend each month. When I'm bored, you'll leave."

It didn't take long for Shane to weigh matters and agree to her terms. Soon he was taking a tour of the carriage house with Hazel.

"So you see," said his new landlady, "It's a good size, just shy of 1500 square feet. Two bedrooms, pool room, your own laundry, completely furnished, all linen, dishes, pantry is stocked, and Fritz will bring fresh groceries each week."

Again, Shane could barely speak.

"Fritz?"

"The chef. He likes to experiment with different meals each week, so he might ask if you'll try them out. Oh yes, you can have use of the pool and tennis courts."

Hazel faced Shane and noticed he was breathing funny.

"Are you okay?"

He sat down on the nearest chair.

"I just realized what the odd feeling is that I've been having lately," he gasped.

Hazel was intrigued. "Tell me!" she said enthusiastically.

Shane took in a deep breath and let it out slowly.

"I'm homesick."

Hazel patted his knee gently. "Welcome home," she said sweetly, then added, "At least until I get bored."

That night, Shane Mitchell walked around and around his new home. He loved it. He also started making notes. He had a good forty years of material but telling about his deceptive deeds would take a lot less time than it actually took to live them. Shane was not deterred. He figured if he stretched things out, he could live on Hazel's property for at least ten years.

By that time, he should be in her will.

Gore in the *Garden*

How to Water Your Garden by Kicking the Bucket

"I want you to read this," Tracy insisted as she put the newspaper over Maureen's cereal bowl.

Maureen put on her readers and said aloud, "For all your massage needs contact Candy. I'm as sweet as can be." She removed the newspaper from her breakfast and grabbed the brown sugar.

"I don't actually need a massage right now; I just want to eat my breakfast in peace."

"Oh for heaven's sake Mother, the ad I've circled!" protested Maureen's twelve-year-old daughter. "Here let me read it to you." She read:

"Did you do something bad, but can't quite remember? Did your neighbor do something bad, and you want to get the goods on them? Contact Gracie Noseworthy Investigations at 555-2368. I sniff out trouble!"

"We should contact this Gracie and tell her about Grandpa!"

Shelley Dawn Siddall

Maureen ate in silence while trying to figure out how best to let her daughter down easy. Maureen's Dad had died one year ago to the day and Tracy was sure he had been murdered by his new wife.

"I know you loved your Grandpa hon and miss him like crazy. But I also know that the police went through everything and declared his death an accident." She looked at her daughter who was staring at her feet. "Anniversaries are hard, aren't they?"

"Damn straight."

"Tracy! Language please."

"Mom, let me phone and talk to this Gracie Noseworthy."

Maureen sighed. Her flakes were soggy.

"On two conditions. One, you will pay for the investigator out of your savings. Two, any interviews will need to be held here at our home with me present."

"Oh Mom, you'll ruin it. You'll tell the police side of things and tell her to go away!"

"I promise to keep my mouth shut."

Tracy had already dialed the number. She had the phone up to her ear when she said to her mother, "I decided I don't want a scooter anyhow if I have to wait years until I'm old enough to drive it. I have lots of money in my savings account already so I can pay the investigator and still have money left over to buy a keyboard."

"Well that's a good instrument to learn to play the piano on. Mind you, if you intend to teach, you will eventually need a musical instrument acceptable to the Royal Conservatory of Music," Gracie said.

"What?" Tracy said.

Maureen whispered, "Manners."

"Hi, I'm Tracy Smiley. What do you charge to investigate a murder, please?"

"Hi Tracy. I'm Gracie Noseworthy. I charge one hundred dollars, if and only if I think there is a case."

Gore in the *Garden*

"One hundred dollars a day?" Tracy was shocked.

"No Tracy; I enjoy investigating, so I charge one hundred dollars overall plus any expenses. You do sound younger than my average client. Is it okay with your parents if you hire me?"

"It's just my Mom and me. She's sitting right here, but she promised to keep her trap shut, so she can't talk to you."

Maureen grabbed the phone. "Hi Gracie. This is Tracy's mom Maureen. I agreed not to say anything about the background of the death Tracy would like you to investigate. I would like any meetings to be held at my home though."

"No worries Maureen. This being Saturday, I assume Tracy is out of school. Can we meet in an hour?"

***

In preparation for the Private Investigator's visit, Tracy had changed her outfit and her hair several times. She was currently wearing green checkered leggings, a long black tunic, and a short jean vest. Her hair had been sprayed and teased but was pulled back in a simple ponytail.

Maureen felt a pang of sadness. Her little girl was growing up. Was I ever that fashion conscious at that age, she wondered. Nope, not even close.

The doorbell rang. Tracy quickly slipped her stocking feet into a pair of black lace up ankle boots and raced to the door.

"Impressive," she said to Gracie Noseworthy.

As the client and the investigator came into the living room, Maureen could not believe what she was looking at.

An older woman, quite beautiful, with long silver hair in a simple ponytail entered with Maureen's daughter. Of course this was Gracie Noseworthy, but the surprising thing was her outfit.

Gracie was wearing green leggings, a black tunic, a jean vest, and lace-up ankle boots.

Gracie broke the ice. "Good to know I dress like a fourteen-year-old," she said with a chuckle.

"I'm only twelve and I think you look stylin'." Tracy pulled out a notebook. "Shall we go over my notes?"

Maureen stifled a giggle.

"One year ago today, my Grandpa, Robert Smiley died. I think it was murder and let me tell you why. He always put his garden hose away and this time he didn't. He always would turn the tap off then spray out the rest of the water until the hose curled up and then put it in a plastic bucket." Tracy set her jaw. "People who say it was an accident are just stupid!"

Gracie took Tracy seriously and opened her own notepad. "And if it is not too painful, Tracy, can you tell me how your Grandpa died?"

"Well, the police say it was an accident, but obviously I don't think so. He was out in the morning really early watering his garden. For some reason he had to go down to the basement and when he got there he slipped in some water, fell down and drown."

"Drown?" Gracie asked.

"Yes. They say he accidentally kicked the bucket, knocked it over, and broke the basement window. They say he went into the basement to pick up the pieces of glass, but he forgot to turn off the tap and all this water ran into the basement." Tracy read something in her notebook. "Did you know you can drown in four inches of water? I didn't believe it at first, but it's true, I looked it up."

"Why do you want to re-investigate now? Has anything happened this year, or even this week that makes your Grandpa's death more suspicious?"

Gore in the *Garden*

Tracy glanced at her Mom. "It's Grandpa's wife. She makes the most terrible jokes about Grandpa. I get the reference to 'kicking the bucket' but it's sick the way she laughs about it."

"She always makes that joke," Maureen said.

"Mom! You said you'd be quiet!"

"Sorry."

Gracie and Maureen exchanged a knowing look. "Please go on, Tracy. What else is bothering you?"

Tracy's lower lip trembled. "I didn't tell you this before Mom, but I heard Sheree..." Tracy explained, "That's Grandpa's wife. Anyway, I heard Sheree telling someone at the grocery store, "Yeah my husband got hosed!" And then the person said, "Was that before or after he got life insurance?" And Sheree said, "Definitely after!" and then she laughed in that sick way she does."

Gracie felt sad. It did sound like Sheree Smiley wasn't a nice person, but it didn't sound like murder. Tracy was staring earnestly at Gracie. Poor kid. "Anything else?" Gracie asked.

"Sheree's friend then said, "Was that before or after he found out about you and the trainer?" And Sheree says, "Coincidentally, not too long after."

Gracie wrinkled her forehead. "I'm just not seeing any evidence of foul play here, Tracy. Sure, it sounds like this Sheree is a rotter, and is treating your Grandpa's memory scandalously, but I can't take your money."

Tracy burst into tears and threw her notebook on the floor. Gracie reached down to pick it up and noticed the drawings on the inside.

"What's this?"

The young girl sniffed, then went and sat beside Gracie.

"This is experiment I did at Grandpa's yesterday. Yes Mom, I know I was supposed to be in school, but I had two study periods and biology. I'm acing biology anyway. Sheree said I could water the garden if I wanted to. She doesn't take care of it, but a lot of his perennial flowers are still living because we had such a rainy spring. Oh, and his strawberries!"

Gracie tapped the page. "Is this the window?"

"Yup. See, Grandpa had a system. First he'd water the flowers in the front yard, then the flowers and veggies in the back." Tracy confided, "Grandpa always said he liked to water the plants himself, but Mom and I think he was too cheap to put in an underground sprinkler system. Anyway, after he watered everything, now this is important, he would go and turn the tap off. Then, he would water the little red maple which is right across from the tap. He would do that until the hose shrunk and then plop the hose in the plastic bucket. There is no way that hose could break the window."

Gracie raised her eyebrows. "How does a garden hose shrink?"

"He had one of those new ones that expand when you turn the water on. I measured it yesterday. The original size is fifty feet, but it expands to three times that size when the water is turned on. Grandpa always kept his in a bucket because you're supposed to keep it out of the sun; it says so in the instructions."

"I've seen them advertised on TV." Gracie rubbed her jaw. "But I'm just not getting the picture. Look, I think a field trip is called for. I have underground irrigation in my backyard, but I have been thinking of getting one of those hoses for all my hanging plants. Let's go get one, no expense to you and we can re-enact your Grandpa's watering routine at my place."

Maureen and Tracy were ready to go in minutes. As they piled into Gracie's silver car, Tracy said approvingly, "Lux."

"I take it that's a good thing?" Gracie whispered to Maureen.

Maureen nodded, but then whispered a warning, "Don't be surprised if you get mistaken for her Mother because you're dressed the same."

Gracie said in the same quiet tone, "It would be an honor." Gracie then raised her voice and addressed Tracy in the backseat, "My car will not start until everybody does up their seatbelts."

"Really?" Maureen whispered.

Tracy leaned forward and whispered between the two women, "No Mom, she's just saying that, so we'll do up our seatbelts. I have excellent hearing you know. You can stop your whispering already."

Gracie started the car and then said in a loud whisper to Maureen, "Do you think she can still hear us?"

"Oh I doubt it."

Tracy yelled from the backseat. "I'm rolling my eyes I'll have you know!"

***

The trio by-passed going through Gracie's house and went straight to the back yard. The new fifty-foot garden hose was attached to the tap.

"Don't turn the water on!" Tracy yelled as she looked for a bucket. Gracie opened her garden shed and let Tracy look around.

"This is exactly the same one Grandpa had!"

It was a large orange bucket Gracie had bought from the hardware store. Tracy put the coiled hose inside the bucket and directed Gracie to turn the water on.

The hose rapidly expanded and filled up the bucket.

"It looks like it's alive!" said Maureen.

"It's going to tip the bucket over, watch out!" said Gracie, stepping out of the way.

Tracy didn't move. "Nope, it won't."

The bucket didn't tip over.

"See!" the tween said victoriously. "Even if the water was on and the hose was in the bucket, it wouldn't tip over. Now, let's look at how Grandpa always did things. Watch."

Tracy took the bucket and dumped the expanded hose out on the sidewalk. "Let's pretend I'm going to water your garden, so I'll drag this way out here."

Gracie could see the girl struggling to gather up the water laden loops of the hose.

"Now, turn the tap off please Mom. Okay, thanks. You're set-up is different, but this is what Grandpa would do. Can I just water this grass?"

"Oh sure," said Gracie. She watched as Tracy started to drain the hose. The hose started to shrink so Tracy walked closer and closer to Gracie and Maureen.

Tracy easily picked up the contracted hose and plopped it in the bucket.

"Grandpa always did it this way. Do you understand now?" she asked.

Gracie nodded. "Even if he, for some unknown reason, suddenly turned the hose back on after he had drained it, the bucket wouldn't tip over and break the window. If he had left the water turned on, the hose would already be in great loops on the ground so it wouldn't suddenly move and break a window."

Tracy was nodding but then stopped and snapped her fingers. "Here's something I never thought of before." She went over to the hose, picked up the nozzle and pointed it at Gracie. "Why did the hose stay on?"

"Oh that's easy," said Maureen. "You just flick that little metal thing over and it will stay on and keep spraying so your hand doesn't cramp up."

"No kidding Mom, but the police said the basement was flooded with water after the window broke. So what did Grandpa

Gore in the *Garden*

do in the meantime? Just stand there watching the basement fill up? It would have taken some time."

Maureen looked at Gracie. "Dad had all his marbles. It doesn't make any sense that he would just stand around for what, five hours or more?" She stopped talking and looked at her daughter in amazement.

"You're right honey. We have to go to the police!"

***

Ted and Gracie were enjoying a perogy dinner at his place.

"I looked into Sheree Smiley. She's a piece of work, that one. Do you know she sued her personal trainer for 'failure to comply with the terms of the contract' or some such nonsense? The small claims court transcript made for some interesting reading."

Gracie put a huge dollop of sour cream to her mound of perogies and onions. She then dumped even more grated cheese and green onions on top. After a satisfying mouthful, she said, "What was his defense? She asked me to have an affair with her instead?"

"Yup. He also said he was just supposed to keep billing her so her husband wouldn't get suspicious. But onto this garden hose business; that Tracy Smiley is a right smart little girl to have figured it all out!"

"And why didn't you?"

"Heah, it wasn't even my case! Although I shouldn't talk against my brothers in blue, they really should have caught the discrepancy in the time it would take to fill up the basement with water."

"I guess you could calculate that. Let's see the square footage of the flooded basement multiplied by the depth of the water would give you the cubic feet. So let's say his house was 1400 square feet and the report said there was about four inches of water?"

"Oh my goodness Gracie, are you going to do math at dinner? I am impressed. Actually, what is really impressing me is the amount of food you can eat and still stay so slim."

Gracie laughed. "No I could only get part way with that calculation. Forget the math. Let's think of a pool. It takes hours to fill a pool with a garden hose. Wouldn't an entire basement with four inches of water be somewhat comparable to a residential pool full of water?"

"That it would. Like I said, the cops that handled this case last year really dropped the ball. I wonder why? Now with this timeline restructured, the whole report Sheree gave is suspect."

"Pass the garlic bread please. What did Sheree say happened?"

"As you can imagine, the report was scanty. It read something like, 'Wife said she was out at the Legion, handling the meat lottery and when she came home, her husband was dead in the basement, she called 911 immediately'. Yes, this is one case I'll be handling personally. I don't know how will be able to prove Sheree murdered him though."

Gracie was thoughtful. "Let me look up something," she said.

The couple had a rule, no cell phones during meal times. This was an exception. Gracie tapped on her phone.

"Ah ha! Guess what day he died on?" She didn't wait for a reply. "It was a Wednesday. The meat lottery at the Legion is on Tuesdays. Trudy-Faye is there every Tuesday and usually wins something, you know, ribs or a roast."

Ted smiled. "This is a good start."

Gracie started to get into the case. "And check the autopsy for contusions to the back of the head and…"

Ted interrupted. "My dear, can we finish our meal first and then discuss heads being bashed in? I think you're going to like dessert. It's green and sounds like pistachio-mint ice-cream with chocolate sauce."

"Hmm, with such a vague description as that I wonder what it could be?"

***

Zoey was not talking to Gracie. Gracie stared at her little cat and tried not to laugh. Zoey was sitting on the washing machine in her cute little pink tutu and matching pink nail caps; but she was seething with anger. Her eyes were hooded, and she hissed at Gracie.

Her human had been away most of the afternoon and well into the evening and Zoey was having a hissy fit.

Of course, a few minutes before the cats heard the car in the drive, they had been playing a wonderful game of "I'm going to rip your head off if you keep chasing me; no, I'm going to rip your head off if you keep chasing me."

Gracie knew she was faking it. And she knew how to prove it.

"Boy, I have so many notes to type up!"

Zoey's eyes got rounder at the word type. She dropped her head and watched as Gracie turned on the computer. Gracie reached in a drawer, pulled out two boxes and set them up to the left of the computer. In a flash, Zoey was on the desk and in one of the boxes.

Frank was busy attempting to climb inside the ankle boots Gracie had kicked off at the door, but when he heard Gracie start to type, he launched himself towards the desk. Speed he had, agility, not so much. He completed an almost perfect somersault then hopped onto the desk and into the box beside Zoey. Both cats sat with their heads angled towards the screen. They loved to watch Gracie's fingers and to check her typing for spelling mistakes.

"So I'm Robert Smiley. I've just finished watering my garden, draining the hose, and carefully storing it away, and now what do I do? Do I sit around the house watching baseball and fail to notice my wife creeping outside then breaking out a window and filling up the basement with water?"

Zoey yowled.

"Yea, I'm not fond of that idea either. The timeline just doesn't work. Robert's body was found around one in the afternoon." Gracie decided to make a pot of coffee. The cats followed her into the kitchen to help and possibly convince her to give them a snack. Gracie needed to fire up her brain cells. With a cup in hand, she returned to the desk and the cats hopped in the boxes again. Inspiration struck immediately.

"How about this, what if Sheree filled up the basement the evening before?"

Frank sat up straighter. His opened his mouth and his lower jaw began quivering. He made an insistent chirping noise.

"I think we have a winner!" Gracie said happily. "So, Robert goes out to water Wednesday morning, he sees the window already broken and the garden hose shoved through it. Says something like, 'what the hell' and goes into the basement to investigate. Sheree is waiting with, hmm a blunt instrument, bonks him on the head and leaves him in the water to drown."

Gracie had been typing this idea under theory as she spoke to the cats. They were fascinated.

"Now what did Sheree do? She wasn't at the meat lottery. Ted said she doesn't work, so what would a cold-hearted woman do while her husband was dying? She had to kill time while she was killing her husband."

Gracie tapped her chin. The cats were bored because she had stopped typing, so they began a boxing match while sitting in their respective boxes. Gracie watched as they batted one another; their little paws paddling away in the air.

"That's it!" she said. "Sheree loves rotten puns. I think she is the type of woman who would have gone swimming while her husband was drowning!"

Gracie started typing a to do list in earnest. She had to check the day of the regular meat lottery at the local legion; was it really Tuesday? Did the neighbors hear the sound of glass breaking Tuesday night? Did the Smiley's have an on-line utility account that would show their daily water usage? Did anyone see Sheree at the Huckleberry pool Wednesday morning?

Gracie had a sick thought. Did Sheree take pictures?

"I am going to talk to Ted first thing in the morning; maybe he can get a search warrant for her phone."

Gracie shut down the computer. "Time for bed kids!" As the cats raced to the bedroom, Gracie collapsed the boxes and filed them away.

That night she dreamed of a large needle. This is going to be easy to thread she thought. The needle turned upside down, grew larger and morphed into a noose. Gracie put the thread through the noose with ease.

"Gotcha!" she said, then rolled over and slept soundly the rest of the night.

***

Tracy had decided to go undercover. Sunday morning she drove her bicycle over to Sheree's house.

"Well what brings you by so early in the morning munchkin? Come on in, have a cup of coffee."

"Is anybody else here?" Tracy asked as her eyes darted around the kitchen.

"Like my latest lover? Oh, don't pretend you haven't thought that! What do you take in your coffee munchkin? Oh never mind; I'll make you a special flavored one. You'll love it."

Tracy was torn. She didn't know what to talk about first; the fact that she hated being called munchkin, that she wasn't even thinking about a lover, um, gross and that she wanted cream and sugar in her coffee. She remembered something she read in a book about how to make friends. She had to show interest in what they were interested in.

"Just came by to hang and um drink coffee. What are you up to these days?"

Sheree looked at Tracy sideways. The older woman shook her head as if to dismiss a thought and smiled at the young girl. "Well you know, with this little bit of money I now have, I've been doing stuff I've always wanted to do."

"Yeah? Like what?"

"I bought one of those paddle boards and I'm going to start lessons on Tuesday!" Sheree said excitedly.

"What, and miss the meat lottery at the legion?"

"Now how do you know that missy?" Sheree demanded.

Tracy had never lied so fast in her life. "I went on-line and searched the photos for pictures of Grandpa. I just happened to notice under events it had 'meat lottery' on Tuesdays." Tracy shrugged her shoulders. "That's all."

Sheree relaxed. "It's not like I'm on the executive or anything. I just help out collecting tickets and things like that. What are you supposed to be doing, Tracy? Don't you have homework or something?"

Tracy shrugged again. "Nah. I'm a brain. So what else have you been doing?"

"Well, you know I loved your Grandpa, but I am dating."

Tracy wanted to puke. Fortunately, her cell phone rang.

Gore in the *Garden*

"Tracy Lisette Smiley, where are you?"

"Hi Mom. I'm over visiting with Sheree."

"You get home right now. I need you at home right now. Please."

Tracy was alarmed. Her Mom sounded really worried.

"Bye Sheree, I've got to go home. Thanks for the coffee!"

"But you didn't even drink any of it and I made it special for you, like a fancy coffee shop coffee. Here, just take a sip!"

Without thinking Tracy reached out her hand to take the mug. An adult was telling her to do something, so she was on automatic pilot. Through the window behind Sheree, she could see Grandpa's huge orange poppies swaying in the slight breeze.

Wait, this woman killed Grandpa, Tracy told herself as her eyes locked with Sheree's.

Sheree was smiling; her eyes were glittering.

Tracy turned and ran out the door. She hopped on her bike and was pedaling so fast she had to keep changing the gears as she flew along the streets of town. Along the way, she determined that she would never go undercover again!

When she rounded the corner to her home, she saw her Mom standing on the sidewalk.

Maureen hugged her daughter and started crying.

"Are you okay Tracy? What did she do to you? Did you eat or drink anything while you were there? Oh my gosh Tracy don't you ever go near that woman again!"

"No worries, Mom. I'm only twelve so I don't have womanly intuition yet, but I think she was going to kill me."

Mother and daughter hugged it out on the sidewalk and then walked slowly back to their house, rolling Tracy's bike as they went. It was then Tracy noticed Gracie Noseworthy's car parked by the curb.

"Is Gracie here with news?" Tracy asked her Mom as she locked up her bike.

Gracie was standing in the living room and spontaneously hugged Tracy when she came in the door.

"Are you okay? Did you eat or drink anything at Sheree's?"

Tracy looked back and forth at her Mom and Gracie.

"Okay, what's going on?"

Maureen let out a big breath. "I've got to sit."

"Let's all sit," Gracie said.

"Okay, we're all sitting," Tracy announced with a false bravado. She was still pretty scared. There was something about the smile Sheree had given her and the look in her eyes. Tracy thought she could see some crazy there mixed with evil bitch. At that thought, Tracy started to blush and looked down at her feet.

Gracie tented her fingers, while Tracy and Maureen continued to hold hands as they sat close to one another on the couch.

"Let's go over this slowly, it's a bit complicated. Mind you Tracy is the one that figured out the garden hose situation, so I'm sure you'll be able to follow along. Item one; did you know Tracy, that you were in your Grandpa's will?"

"He asked me if I would like his garden and I said sure! But I figured once he married Sheree, she would get the garden."

"There was a will," Gracie explained, "leaving the house, garden, everything to you, with the inheritance to be managed by your Mom until you reached legal age. Now this will was dated two years before he married Sheree; you would have been about eight I guess?"

Maureen and Tracy nodded.

"Your Grandpa did not change this will, however, the law states a lot of mumbo jumbo, but basically, he could not leave his wife destitute."

Gore in the *Garden*

Maureen had talked briefly to Gracie about this, but hearing it again, she was so disappointed. Tracy would have loved to work in her Grandpa's garden. It would help her with her grief. Plus it would have been nice to have their own home rather than renting.

Gracie checked her phone. "Sorry, I don't mean to be rude, but I'm just waiting for a message from Detective Bailey. So you don't get the house, despite the will. Now then, the Detective I mentioned is a personal friend of mine…" Gracie shook her head and continued, "Oh for heaven's sake, he's my boyfriend and when we had dinner last night I told him about this case."

Tracy wasn't grossed out to learn that Gracie was dating and was actually pretty happy it was a policeman.

"Unbeknownst to me, he made a lot of phone calls last night and this morning. Last night, he woke up Mr. Carlson owner and agent of Munson Insurance Agency and had a discussion with him. This brings us to item two."

Tracy tried to get up, but her Mom held onto her.

"I need some water Mom; I rode like a bat out of hell to get away from that woman!"

Maureen was just so pleased her daughter was safe, that she didn't even chide her for her language. Tracy gulped down a glass of water and then brought in a pitcher of water for her Mom and Gracie.

"Item two is life insurance. Again, Tracy was the beneficiary."

Tracy frowned. "But Sheree told me this morning that she had come into money; so did Grandpa change the beneficiary?"

"Hold onto your hats, but in a way, Sheree did."

Maureen said, "I'm confused. I thought only the policy holder could do that?"

Gracie took a sip of water. "So this is where it gets a bit complicated. Sheree talked your Grandpa into raising the amount of the life insurance. Because the beneficiary did not change, Mr.

Carlson could receive verbal instructions from your Grandpa to increase the payout."

Gracie looked at Maureen and Tracy. "Mr. Carlson confirmed that he knew your Grandpa; he knew his voice and indeed, the life insurance policy was increased about one month before your Grandpa died. He told Mr. Carlson on the phone that his wife suggested the increased amount. Only one premium was paid for the new amount. In cases like this, where there is a substantial increase in the life insurance and the policy holder suddenly dies, an investigation is automatically initiated."

"So Mr. Carlson was already investigating Grandpa's death?"

"Yes, but as the saying goes, all the t's were crossed, and all the i's were dotted."

"But we didn't get any money," Tracy lamented, "and I need braces, and the landlord is dragging his feet about fixing the roof…"

Her Mom patted her hand. "We'll make do. It's my job to worry about that stuff, not yours. It will be fine. Let's listen to Gracie."

"Onto item three. Did you know that one Maureen Angela Smiley went into Munson Insurance Agency and picked up a check for fifty thousand dollars approximately three months after a death certificate was mailed to Mr. Carlson?"

Maureen threw her hands in the air. "What? I did nothing of the sort!"

"You know that, and I know that, but Mr. Carlson said the woman who came to pick up the check in trust for her daughter, had ID stating she was Maureen Angela Smiley. He gave her the check."

At that moment, Gracie's phone beeped. She looked at it and smiled broadly.

Gore in the *Garden*

"And Constable Dave is in Munson. He informed Detective Bailey that Mr. Carlson has just identified a photo of Sheree Smiley as the person who picked up the check!"

Tracy pumped her fist in the air. "Whoo hoo! I can get braces!"

"Said no regular child ever," Maureen smirked. "My girl has a fascination with dentistry."

"I want to operate on children with cleft palates and stuff, like they do on that TV show. For free of course. But I'll have to have regular patients first in order to do the free stuff."

Gracie could feel tears starting to well up. "You are a remarkable young girl and kudos to you Mom, for raising such a fine daughter on your own!"

Gracie had even more good news for the family, but she wanted to continue with several points first. She wanted to make sure they understood how the murder investigation was progressing.

"Item four, with this confirmation of fraud, Sheree will now be picked up by the police."

"Right now?" Tracy asked. When Gracie nodded, Tracy did another fist pump in the air.

"Can you phone your boyfriend and have him look for that coffee she made for me? I think there was something wrong with it."

Gracie hit Ted's number immediately.

"Ted, are you at Sheree's home? There might be poison in a coffee cup." Gracie asked Tracy. "What did the mug look like?"

Tracy yelled toward the phone, "It was the bear mug. The one that says an old bear lives here with his honey."

"Did you hear that Ted? Okay good. I think she tried to poison Tracy. Is that her screaming? Yikes. Someone should wash her mouth out with soap. Talk to you later."

"And finally we are at item five. I'm sorry to tell you that there isn't enough evidence, yet, to prove that Sheree murdered your Grandpa."

Everyone sighed at the same time.

Gracie hugged Maureen. "Sorry to leave on such a depressing note, but I have a few more things to look into." She turned to Tracy. "And you, young lady, will have to write me a check for one hundred dollars once you have some money."

"Nope, I'll give it to you right now." Tracy went to her backpack and pulled out five wrinkled twenties from her donut shaped pink change purse.

"Right, and I'll make up a receipt and give it to you this evening along with a further report."

***

Gracie's afternoon was spent shopping. She went shopping for a one-month swim pass at the Huckleberry pool where she found out that they had no way of tracking drop-ins at the pool; she went shopping for a personal trainer at 'buns-r-us' and she went shopping for a house.

A very friendly looking woman opened the door.

"Yes?"

"Hi. I'm Gracie Noseworthy. I live over on Landsbury Lane but was thinking about re-locating to this neighborhood. All the homes here seem to have a lot of land and beautiful gardens. Do you like living here? Is it a safe neighborhood would you say?"

The woman narrowed her eyes.

"I know you." She pointed a flour cover finger at Gracie.

Gracie was certain she had not met her before.

Gore in the *Garden*

The woman left the doorway and walked inside. She hollered back to Gracie, "I'm just making some dill and cheese biscuits. Come on in and we can talk about your latest case."

Have I lost a marble, or two, Gracie wondered as she followed the woman inside. No. I definitely do not know this woman. How does she know me and how does she know I'm on a case?

"I'm Joyce. I see your ad in the paper all the time and recognized your name. I was actually thinking about phoning you last year; but the police said everything was fine."

If it wouldn't have been so obvious, Gracie would have slapped herself on the forehead. Of course. Her ad.

"Boy, this is quite the operation you have going here! What's the occasion?"

"I'm President of the Neighborhood Watch, so I'm making a few dozen biscuits for the potluck tonight. That yard over there," she pointed a thumb to the window where brilliant orange poppies celebrated the sun, "had a few cop cars show up this morning. They drug the widow out in handcuffs! So the neighbors are naturally upset that they missed something; oh not the show, but the reason behind the show."

Gracie lowered her voice and adopted a confidential tone. "I am working with the police on the Smiley case. What can you tell me about her and why were you going to phone me last year?"

Joyce had finished patting the dough. She floured a little tin circle and began cutting out the biscuits.

"I just use a mini tuna tin for my cookie cutter, or in this case, my biscuit cutter. I opened it on both sides; took the lids off. It's the perfect size." She stopped and looked at Gracie. "Listen, I'll tell you what I know, if you tell me what you know. Deal?"

Gracie needed information. "Deal," she said, "but you first."

"I knew Robert and Shelia Smiley for years. Shelia was the first, and in my opinion, only Mrs. Smiley. They moved in about twenty years ago when their little daughter Maureen was about nine and made a right little paradise of the place. Poor Mo got herself knocked up by some ne'er do well when she was just sixteen and had a little girl."

The stove buzzer sounded to indicate the oven had pre-heated. Joyce popped two trays of biscuits in the over and set the timer for twelve minutes.

"Mo called the little girl Tracy Lisette. Pretty little thing and sharp as a tack! They're living in East Huckleberry and doing okay. Maureen is working for the telephone company and Tracy is a straight A student. Shame about Robert. The night before he died I saw a couple of people out in the backyard; that's why I was going to phone you."

"Why was that suspicious?"

"Shelia died when Mo was fifteen. Mo and her Dad would garden for hours together, but after she had the baby and moved out, she had to have her own place in order to collect welfare, nobody went in that back yard except Robert. Eventually little Tracy would come over and garden with her Grandpa. When the new Mrs. Thing moved in, she didn't give a hoot about gardening. So when I saw two adults out there at night, I opened my window and yelled, "Who's there?". Even though it was nearly summer and of course, it stays light pretty late, I couldn't see them because of the shadow from the house."

Gracie was intrigued. Two people? "What happened?"

"It was that Sheree who yelled back at me; I'd recognize that cackle anywhere. She laughed and said, "Oh Mrs. Hamilton, it's just me! I'm working out here on a surprise for Robert." Well, I knew I saw two people, so I yelled right back, who's there with you? Some male says, "Oh Mrs. Hamilton, it's just me! I'm working with Sheree on a surprise for Robert."

"Did you recognize the voice?"

Gore in the *Garden*

"No, I sure didn't, but I think I would if I ever heard it again. He seemed to have an accent of some sort; I couldn't quite place it. Then I heard something like glass breaking, so I called out again, "Everything all right over there?" And that sarcastic male says, "Oh Mrs. Hamilton why don't you mind your own beeswax!" I thought it odd, especially when Robert died the next day, but the police ruled it an accident. I bet it wasn't though. Is that why you're here?"

Gracie nodded. "There's only so much I can say. But I wonder if you could tell all this to the police?"

"Of course I'll tell the police if you think I should, but we had a deal Gracie Noseworthy! You've got to tell me more than that."

"The dear widow stole the granddaughter's money. Sheree used forged ID, pretended she was Maureen and collected the life insurance check meant for Tracy! All fifty thousand dollars of it!"

"No!" gasped Joyce Hamilton.

In spite of herself, Gracie loved spilling the details. "But do you want to know something that even Maureen and Tracy don't know?"

Joyce said "Of course!" as the timer sounded on the stove. She put trivets on the counter and slammed the two trays of perfectly browned baking powder biscuits down. "Go!" she ordered Gracie.

"The life insurance policy was one of those installment ones. So Tracy would get a certain sum every year, of course to be managed by her Mom, instead of one huge sum."

"That is fantastic news. Do you realize what this means? Tracy's going to University to become some sort of dental surgeon!"

Joyce buttered two biscuits and set them before Gracie.

"You'll need a coffee to go with that. So what happened this morning?"

"Well, Sheree was arrested for fraud. Plus, they are waiting lab results on a coffee she was trying to get Tracy to drink. I think somehow in Sheree's twisted brain she figured if she got rid of the real beneficiary of the life insurance policy, then she'd be home free. But here's the really big news. It's not public knowledge yet so..."

"You got it Gracie; I won't say anything. Maybe I better cancel that meeting tonight, so I don't inadvertently spill the beans!"

"No, I think you're going to be the star of the meeting with the inside track. It will be public knowledge this afternoon. Sheree Smiley was also charged with the murder of her husband Robert Smiley."

"No!" Joyce gasped.

"Yes. And her co-conspirator, Danny Lachman was charged as well. He was none other than her personal trainer! Apparently, Sheree had sued him on some pretense, then to make it up to him, convinced him to help her kill her husband and she would split the life insurance money with him."

"Was he quite a bit younger than her? I mean, he told me to mind my own beeswax. It sounded like an immature thing to say."

Gracie drank her cup of coffee and told Joyce about her search for a personal trainer that afternoon. Gracie did not tell Joyce that Ted had told her the trainer's name was Danny Lachman and Gracie had agreed to do a bit of undercover work at the gym. As directed, Gracie told Danny during their interview, that Sheree Smiley had recommended him, and did you hear Sheree had received over a million dollars in a life insurance pay out last year?

Gracie also did not tell Joyce that yes Danny was young but was terribly good looking in a muscular tanned kind of way. If you liked that sort of thing.

"So Danny went to complain to the police that he had helped Sheree kill her husband and he didn't even get his fair share of the money promised him."

Gore in the Garden

"Poor thing," said Joyce, "I imagine the police patted his hand and told Sheree to give him the money."

"Not quite," laughed Gracie. "The way I heard it; Danny was perplexed when he was arrested. He kept insisting Sheree owed him money and the police should arrest her for theft." Gracie smiled wryly. "He was assured several times that Sheree was already arrested, and she would be charged with murder. Danny probably still doesn't understand that when you confess to murder, that rather trumps any complaints you might have."

"So who's moving in next to me?" Joyce wondered. "Please don't tell me Sheree has a sister!"

"Maureen and Tracy! They inherit everything now!"

"How flipping fantastic! Oh that yard is going to be breathtaking again once those two work their magic on it!"

Gracie put Joyce's number in her phone and promised to call her when everything was public knowledge. When Joyce found out Gracie was headed over to Maureen's, she made Gracie promise to give them her love.

After Gracie left, Joyce received a phone call she was rather expecting. It was the receptionist from 'buns r us' telling Joyce that, regretfully, her personal training session with Danny Lachman was cancelled and that he would not be available for the foreseeable future.

Joyce sat down and ate three more biscuits. She would start her diet tomorrow.

Shelley Dawn Siddall

A Garden Party for Death

She sat at her tidy desk, elegantly addressing invitations. The calligraphy pen was a gift from a long-ago suitor who had died under mysterious circumstances. She only used it for very special occasions.

"You are formally invited to a garden party for death," she wrote. "You will be one of thirteen attendees and will be called upon to make a short speech about how death influenced the choices you have made in your life. Formal attire is required, and it must be completely black with the exception of a white boutonniere for men and a white corsage for women. Hats are optional.

If they are living at the time, the list of attendees will be as follows:

Mr. Ted Bailey
Mr. Fred Downton
Mr. Byron Eggplant
Mr. Barry Frederickson
Mrs. Trudy-Faye Gervais
Mr. Conrad Jeffries
Mrs. Gracie Noseworthy
Mr. Anderson Payne

Gore in the *Garden*

Mr. Leon Pitre
Miss Barbara Shire
Miss Maureen Smiley
Mrs. Julia Smith
Mrs. Jasmine Summan

She added the address, date and time of the garden party and mailed each invitation in an envelope with black edging.

She neglected to mention that death would be at the garden party as well. After all, it was his party. Or was it her party?

At the appointed time, the garden party took place in the peony garden at the Huckleberry Hospice. The peonies were just about at the end of their season; the gardener had not cut them back yet, so they drooped down and shed their petals like colorful tears.

The table was sparsely set for the party. A white linen tablecloth with thirteen crystal glasses already filled with white wine. A series of white cards were laid out along the length of the table, each elegantly adorned with a number.

Julia Smith was the first to arrive. She wore a thigh length floral lace dress with a miniature top hat perched on her head. Julia's hat had a long train of netting that flowed down her back. She picked up the card with number one calligraphed on it and sat down.

Conrad Jeffries was next. His black suit was expertly tailored and complimented by a beautifully pressed black cotton shirt with a black silk tie. He wore a tiny white rose for his boutonniere. He wondered what number he should pick up when Julia waved her number one card at him. He picked up the card with number two written on it and sat beside Julia.

"Are we allowed to talk?" she asked.

"I don't see why not," he said. "I'm Conrad."

"I'm Julia. I forgot I should be wearing a corsage."

Conrad relished his new life. He was determined to be the gentleman he always dreamed he could be, so he hopped up and went over to a white peony bush and broke off a beautiful bloom.

It seemed to explode in his hands. The white petals fell on his highly polished black shoes and rested there.

Julia was mesmerized. A sweet fragrance was released as the petals fell and Julia wondered if she had ever seen anything more beautiful than this huge man trying to bring her a delicate flower.

She got up and together they looked at the other blooms and gently tapped them for integrity. When they found the perfect blossom they carefully snapped it off the stem.

How to affix it to Julia's wrist?

Conrad ran to his car and returned with a roll of black electrical tape. He wrapped the tape, sticky side out and sat the white peony on top. Julia used her pointer finger, beautifully manicured with a deep charcoal polish, and pressed down. Her corsage was complete.

Trudy-Faye Gervais showed up next, red, and sweating in a too long black velvet gown, with a deep V in the front and a high side slit. She sat down heavily at the table and reached for the number three card. She seemed to be wearing the same tiny white rose on her wrist that Conrad was wearing in his label.

Anderson Payne and Maureen Smiley showed up at the same time and literally bumped heads reaching for the same card. Anderson relinquished his hold on card four and picked up card five. They sat down beside one another and began chatting.

Anderson, determined not to be burned again, opened with, "Do you have a pond in your garden?"

Maureen looked at this funny little man, with his prissy little manners and thought he was precious. He was dressed to the nines in the most elegant of attire but came across as anything but elegant in his conversation. She liked him.

Gore in the *Garden*

"My daughter and I have recently come into money and we are indeed thinking of a pond. Now hold onto your regal hat.."

Anderson was wearing a large top hat and he reached his hands up and held onto it as Maureen went on, "My daughter, Tracy, did a report on Japan and fell in love with their fish. They're called Koi and they come all sorts of colors but we both like the ones that are a little bit different. In fact, both Tracy and I like the ones that are all white with just one red spot on their head."

Anderson Payne thought he was going to cry.

It looked as though Leon Pitre had been crying when he came stumbling into the peony garden. He knocked back his glass of white wine and smiled genially at the other guests.

"Anyone up for a song?" he asked.

Julia gave him card number six and told him she would sing with him later.

Ted and Gracie came to the party arm in arm. She looked stunning in her floor length gown. It had an all lace bodice and matching sleeves. The gown had ruching over one hip and draped beautifully on Gracie's slim figure. Her hair was an up-do with large loops of lace scattered among her curls.

Not to be overlooked was Ted Bailey. He had on a black tuxedo, black shirt and a black cummerbund and bow tie. His chest was puffed out as he escorted Gracie to the table. They were guests seven and eight, respectively.

A titter started rumbling in the group and then became out and out laughter as Barb Shire and Barry Frederickson sauntered in the garden wearing matching outfits. Each had a top hat, a bow tie, a suit jacket, a shirt and a pair of walking shorts and black sneakers. They also carried a fancy walking stick, which they twirled and used to point for no particular reason other than to create more laughter. They also wore the biggest white corsages anyone had ever seen.

They were guests nine and ten.

The next two guests created a stir as well, as their bickering could be heard before they were seen.

Byron Eggplant was fussing over the length of Fred Downton's tie.

"Not past the belt for heaven sakes! Here let me re-tie it."

"Oh stop your fussing. You're like a little old man."

"It's not even a Windsor knot! Here, let me do it."

All bickering stopped when Jasmine Summan walked in. She was determined to wear something as far from her regular scrubs as possible and she succeeded.

She wore a black mermaid dress that had seemingly acres of lace pooled at the bottom. The dress had a sweetheart neckline and hugged her voluptuous figure. It also had tiny sequins that twinkled with every step she took. Every step that was being watched by every person present. She was a dream.

When everyone was seated, Julia held her hand up like a school child. When she was encouraged to speak, she said tentatively, "I have number one, so I guess I give my speech first?"

More nods. She opened her little purse and pulled out some notes.

"I was asleep most of my life until death woke me. It was like waking up to a nightmare. Death took the only people I cared about and thrust me into a life I didn't want. What I wanted was to go back to sleep." She looked at the group. "Death promised that sleep."

Julia shuddered as she thought back. How she sat and read the warning on the box of rat poison. How she decided to try one more time to stand up to Brett before ending her life. How she waited for Brett to come home so she could confront him. But he never did.

Gore in the *Garden*

"And then death changed the rules," she continued. "Death visits you when you least expect it. Death is unpredictable, capricious, sometimes welcomed sometimes not. I am awake now and I do not want to meet death anytime soon. Thank you."

Conrad smiled a quick smiled and showed the other guests his card.

"I'm here tonight to thank death. I didn't know my Mom until she died, and I spent weeks going through her things as I cleared out her house." He cleared his throat several times. "Just as she was trapped inside her disease of mental illness I was trapped inside my anger and resentment. I found many letters and poems she wrote. Most of them didn't make any sense, but some were beautiful. This is one I found with a copy of my Sister's death certificate:

"I wasn't allowed to love you.
they said in whispers only I could hear,
"Don't go near, don't go near."
I wasn't allowed to hug you.
They said I would poison you with my fear,
"Don't go near, don't go near."

Conrad was crying openly now, tears streaming down his face. He took a deep breath and continued,

"And when I die, I'll join you my dear
And I will fight and rage against the whispers,
With my sword I'll protect you my dear
Don't go near, don't go near."

Conrad raised his glass. "So I'd like to thank Death for giving me back my Mom. To death!"

The other twelve raised their glasses and toasted death. Julia poured some of her wine into Mr. Pitre's glass so he could join in the toast.

Shelley Dawn Siddall

Trudy-Faye Gervais looked around the table. She didn't say anything but gripped her wine glass tightly. The silence went on and on. Some present wondered if they should just jump the queue and get their speech over with. Finally Trudy-Faye bellowed, "Death is a jerk," and slammed her wine glass down so hard it broke. She waved away any attempt to help her. "That's it," she said. "Next!"

Maureen said with a giggle, "I guess that's me." She paused and became more somber. "Death made me powerless when my Mom died. Mom was my best friend. I was lost and angry and came up with a plan. I would go out and get pregnant by the first boy that came along and then I would raise that child to be my best friend and I would never let my child out of my sight, ever.

"Somewhere along the line, probably around my second trimester, I realized that I needed grown up friends to help and support me. So I worked hard at being a friend and soon was surrounded with good friends and of course, my number one fan, my Dad. But, like Julia said, Death changed the rules. In one year, two of my friends died of cancer and then my Dad died. But I was determined not to be powerless. I can eat right, exercise, take time to love those precious to me and cherish the memories of those that have died. I can still be afraid of death, but I can be powerful."

"Here, here!" said Ted.

The neatly folded sheets in front of Anderson Payne rippled with a sudden breeze. His hand darted out and held them fast. Carefully, he opened the sheets and began reading from the first one.

"I am not a happy man by nature," he began, "But the one quality that gave me some solace was logic. By happenstance, I saw a blueprint and decided that not only would I pursue drafting, but I would also draft a life plan for myself and then follow it. Logical.

Gore in the *Garden*

"I became like a compass, with one point stuck in a rut, going around and around in the same circle. The death of my marriage knocked me out of one rut and into another. Death has recently visited me again and in so doing, has murdered my apathy. I am now trying new things, new experiences." Anderson raised his eyes and also raised his voice from a monotone recitation of his prepared speech to a spontaneous disclosure.

"I even went on a garden tour!" he said enthusiastically. He carefully tucked his first sheet of paper in his pocket while he held the second sheet securely. The wind was picking up.

"I got the courage to experiment with a type of drawing I always wanted to try." He held up the second sheet that had a black and white finely detailed picture of a fish. "I made this with an old typewriter!"

Maureen reached for the drawing. "It's all letters and brackets and such that somehow make up a fish. Unbelievable! Here, look at this," she said as she handed the drawing across the table to Gracie.

Anderson stood up and reverted to his monotone. "In summation, I did not want to attend this garden party for death. I thought it in poor taste and a waste of time that could be better spent working. But the more I considered the impact death has made in my life, I wanted to let people know, your life will be changed by death. It's evitable and logical. You can however reshape your view of these changes. They can, in fact be positive." He sat down as his drawing went from hand to hand around the table.

"Amazing."

"All this from a typewriter? Hard to believe."

"Look at the detail on the fish scales. Fascinating!"

Julia nudged Leon Pitre. "Your turn."

"My wife wants to kill me, plain and simple." He leaned on the table, his chin in his hand. "I've been a terrible husband, it's true. And speaking of true, I haven't been true to her and she knows it. We fight like cats and dogs. But I always thought it was fun."

"Don't you mean in fun?" Trudy-Faye asked.

"Oh yea, that too," Leon continued. "She'd throw insults at me and I'd throw them right back. It was fun! We did that our whole marriage. Now, a little birdie told me, she's trying to kill me. I can't wrap my brain around it." Leon looked up in the sky. "Here I am death, do your damndest."

"But not anytime soon," Ted said, "I'm off duty."

Everyone laughed.

Ted began his speech without notes. "Death. I've seen a lot of it. The one that impacted me the most was when my Grandma died. I loved her. She was just a little bitty thing. I can still see her standing by the sideboard in her parlor shaking her finger at me and saying, "One day, Theodore, you are going to be old like me and you are going to look back on your life and you are going to ask yourself, "Was I a good person?"

"You see, Grandma had just caught me stealing another piece of her pie. She went on to tell me to take a really hard look at my life and to set goals for myself. "Do something that makes the world a better place," she told me.

"The thing was, I was only eight and I thought she was silly to talk about me being old. I was a kid; I didn't have to think about stuff like goals and jobs for years. She died that week. I wish she could see the direction my life has taken. She would be proud of me, I think."

Gracie reached over and patted his hand in agreement.

"It's interesting, though," Ted added, "She didn't know she was going to die that week, yet she used every day of her life to help instruct and guide others to be a better version of themselves.

Therefore, this is my commitment to intensify my efforts to be a force for good before I am silenced by death."

The breeze had loosened the curls in Gracie hair, and she pushed them out of her eyes.

"Like these curls, death was something to be brushed out of the way. It had never touched me. It was always out there happening to other people," she said with a sad smile. "Until it happened to my late husband. The worst part though, was before he died. It was terrifying to hold in my heart the concept of his impending death. Everything was moving too fast, but at the same time, our life stagnated. We couldn't plan or dream. Everything was on hold while we waited for his death. We would be watching television and see an ad for a dream vacation. Then we would catch that look on each other's face; the wry look of 'not us'.

"After he died; after I rediscovered me, I became a better person. I could understand and empathize with other people's pain to a depth I didn't have before. I cried more often and more easily. I made friends quicker. Some of those bonds have been broken by death. Oddly enough, I now chose to be surrounded by death. I'm not terrified by death any longer. It helps me to separate the dross from the gold."

She started to push her curls out of the way again but stopped and shook her head vigorously. Her curls bounced around her head and gently fell down, framing her face. The pieces of lace lifted with the breeze and danced with the abandoned peony petals.

"Most of what's in my head isn't real," Barbara Shire said. "Ugh, let me start again. This past year I learned that most of what I thought was reality, wasn't. Like Julia, my parents died when I was young. No, that isn't true either. I don't know my parents, never did, but to me, it was as if they died when I was young. I wasn't found on the steps of a church in a basket but just left at the hospital. The woman who birthed me forgot to collect me. She showed up at emergency, gave a false name, had a baby, and left.

"I just invented things all my life and then drifted into believing what I invented. Fortunately, death changed all that. It didn't just rip the bandage off; it tore me apart. I'm still recovering, still working on what's real and what isn't, but I do have a message for everyone. Things can turn out even better than you hoped."

Barry kissed her on the forehead as opposed to her cheek, as Barb had inadvertently burped at the end of her speech.

"I don't have too much to add to what Barb said, except I had the opposite problem. Instead of making up stories in my head and believing them, I just didn't say what was in my head and thought everybody knew what I meant. For example, when I did all those gardening favors for Barb, like pruning her maple, I thought she knew I liked her and wanted to get to know her romantically."

Gracie smirked and looked at Ted. "Who knew?" she asked.

Barb overheard the comment. "Well not me. Not really," she said. "But look at my maple now, it's grown back beautifully!" She passed around her phone opened to several before photos that naturally included Barry, shirtless with a pair of loppers and after photos, of a luxuriant Crimson King maple tree.

Barry continued. "And when my ex-wife kept insisting we get married; in my head I was saying I think it's too soon, but I didn't actually say that, so I just went along with everything. Death made me bolder. Initially I felt such an incredible sense of betrayal, but that quickly changed to fear. Fear that I was going to die without ever having lived."

He turned to Barb who was tucking her phone away in the pocket of her shorts. "Did you hear what I said?"

She looked like she was caught chewing gum in school. "You were frightened you were going to die?" she asked.

Gore in the *Garden*

Barry got up and dropped to one knee. "I said EX-WIFE! Barbara Shire, will you marry me?"

Barb started bawling loudly. "See!" she yelled, "Things turn out even better than you think they will! I thought we were just going to shack up!"

Leon shouted, "Is that a yes woman? If so, say it, the man is breaking his knee for you!"

"YES!"

The couple, naturally, began a passionate embrace until Trudy-Faye barked out, "Oh for Pete's sake, get a room already!"

"I'm number eleven. To break the ice, I'm Byron Eggplant. Yes, I see your raised eyebrows. Eggplant is my last name. I purposely chose that name because I wanted to stand out from the crowd. I'm an author you see and while I've only written one book, well, it's more of a novella, I plan to have a long career as a novelist.

I killed somebody once. It was entirely my fault of course but the police didn't see it that way. They said the person who kidnapped me and stuff, certainly had it coming, and I was just a kid, so at six how did I know how to form the intent or some such phrase, when I plunged the knife in the kidnapper." Byron smoothed his eyebrows and added, "Several times."

The entire garden party seemed to hold their breath, waiting for the rest of the story.

"So yes. Death changed my life. It brought me freedom of a sort; but then I was caged by overprotective parents. Too bad they didn't adopt that role a few months before! But now I'm caged by my own insecurities. I write stuff, but I think it's drivel. So I sought out this famous author; Mr. Fred Downton ladies and gentlemen!"

Fred bowed his head slightly. His wine glass was entirely untouched during the preceding speeches.

"Maybe you've read my book, Grandma's House?" Fred asked. "I see some people nodding. Thank you. But what you probably don't know, is that all those characters in the treatment center were based on one person in my life. Yes, my Mother is the original amalgam of all those twisted personalities. To better understand her, I took her apart, piece by piece.

"I couldn't write the book until she died. In truth, I still haven't written the book I wanted to. Somehow my identity shifted from Frederick, Mommy's little slave to Fred the famous Author. I didn't have an intermediate identity. My current identity is Fred the drunk." He picked up the wine glass and threw the contents out on the ground.

Leon groaned loudly.

Fred Downton continued, "I'm putting you all on notice that I intend to kill Fred the drunk and find Freddy Downton the author." He raised his glass. "To Death; may you find me quickly my friend."

Jasmine's voice could be heard echoing Fred's toast.

"To Death; may you find me quickly my friend," she repeated. "Yes, death and I are old frenemies. Death has eased the suffering of those that are not going quietly into that good night, but death has been known to take young girls before they have even received their first kiss. Death took my little sister when she was just ten. Before she was even out of braids.

"At certain times, I see my little sister's face in every elder I care for.

"I hate death and I will honor her no longer. This party is now over." Jasmine got up, threw her card on the table, and walked out of the garden.

Each of the remaining twelve attendee's threw their card on the table and left the garden without saying a word. Death too left this garden but found another garden close by and lingered.

Gore in the *Garden*

Dropping Beets

Flynn was ecstatic. His new restaurant, Las Vegans, was filling up. Just wait until Liv walked in for her shift; she was going to be totally surprised. He checked his watch and frowned; she was already late.

Who would have thought a little backwater town like Huckleberry would accept a vegan restaurant? Let alone one that was only open for lunch? Let alone one that operated with a restrictive business model!

Las Vegans only allowed twenty-four diners in. Not at a time, but total. Plus, the ones fortunate to be let in for lunch had no say in what they were going to eat. They would eat what they were served.

Of course, it was all organic.

Flynn was stressed. Where the hell was Liv?

"Saffron! I need you to start plating the meal. Can you do that for me?"

Saffron was not amused. She thought this gig would be easy-peasy working for some airy-fairy hipsters but they were, like rude! They wanted the vegetables peeled before they went in the juicer or stew or whatever. And you couldn't even smoke on your break!

That Liv would totally get on your case about contaminating the food with nicotine fingers and nicotine breath.

Saffron was going to go try the burger joint once her friend Nate was the assistant manager. He'd hire her no problem. Working in prep there had to be way easier; everything was frozen.

She stared at the huge pot of roasted butternut squash soup. It actually smelled delish but there was no way she was going to eat here. The great Liv didn't believe in mouse traps; more often than not, Saffron saw a mouse run by. Plus there was poop under the counter where the pots were stored. Saffron even found poop in the pots.

It was no big deal as far as Liv was concerned. She would say, "Let them live their life and we'll live ours." It was gross. The Las Vegans didn't even have bleach on the premises.

Now Flynn wanted her to 'plate the meal'. Saffron was confused.

"You want the soup on a plate?" she asked Flynn.

Flynn picked up a large ceramic bowl with vegetables hand painted on the brim. He filled the bowl with two ladles of soup then swirled coconut 'cream' on top. A fancy 'L' and a fancy 'V' floated across the soup. It was perfection.

"Think you can do that for me?" Flynn asked again.

"Oh sure," Saffron said smiling broadly. As the owner of the cubby-hole restaurant went to the front of the house to check the head count, Saffron dished up the soup. She grabbed the squeeze bottle full of coconut cream, made two dots for eyes and a big smile.

Flynn expected her to serve as well because the great Liv hadn't shown up yet. Saffron wasn't entirely sure of the relationship between them, but Flynn did seem to be the boss. She hoped Liv would really get blasted for being late.

Gore in the *Garden*

***

Liv was actually blasting someone else.

She was in the community garden that she and Flynn had initiated and was giving a piece of her mind to one of the gardeners. They were using insecticide! One of those pump and spray things that sent a fine mist over everything it was aimed at.

"It's drifting on our vegetables, you idiot! Can't you see that? What part of organic do you not understand?"

Leon Pitre had decided to quit drinking and take up gardening. His reasons were two-fold. One, if he stayed sober he could keep an eye on his wife and thwart any attempts she made on his life. And two, gardening in the community garden, was far away from his house and her nagging. He even went out a bought a pair of overalls to work in.

"Now look little lady," Leon said, "I believe the sign says 'Community garden' not organic garden. I happen to like my cabbages moth free!"

"Did you not read our brochure? Pesticides are frowned upon!"

"I'm frowning, I'm frowning!" Leon said with a chuckle while he continued to spray the pesticide on his baby cabbages. He was quite proud of them and quite proud of himself. The only other thing he had successfully planted was Brett Smith under a layer of concrete.

While Liv stewed and mumbled curses, Leon put the sprayer down and sat on the edge of his garden. He had salvaged some wood and built a four-foot square box with a pretty little ledge to sit on. He admired his neat little garden patch and thought about Julia Smith.

She was really blossoming, so perhaps you could say he helped her to grow. It looked like that Conrad Jeffries had taken a shine to her too. Well good for them. It was a pity though, that she would have to wait years before Brett could be declared legally dead. Maybe he shouldn't have buried him so deep?

***

In Liv's former life, she had been a hard driving sales executive in middle management. She was all about the results and her team knew it. They detested her with a passion, but the more she bullied them the more they produced. Their sales numbers were the best in the company. As were their bonuses.

Liv was not only hyper and goal oriented, but she was also sick as a dog. Although she expected everyone around her to jump when she said jump; Liv herself was desk bound and pretty much sedentary. In one year, despite her latest diet, she had gained forty more pounds, her skin was sallow, and she had migraines most days.

Then one day, she ate an organic tomato.

The guy who delivered sandwiches to the office dared her to eat it.

"Bet you have never tasted anything like this in your life!" Flynn had said. "Go on, I dare you!"

She had never tasted anything like that tomato in her entire life. Flynn was right. She was sold.

That began her headlong dive into organic vegetables. She subsequently gave up smoking, eating animals, her job, her apartment, and polyester clothing. She also dropped over a hundred pounds and ran away with Flynn to Huckleberry.

Flynn Tanner and Liv Hayashi moved to town the previous year and found an opportunity. A small restaurant happened to be selling, so they snapped it up to start their own vegan place.

After rather extensive renovations, it was a dream come true. Now, all they needed was a spot to grow their organic vegetables.

Gore in the *Garden*

At the edge of Huckleberry, was a huge building that had been vacant for two years. Apparently, Huckleberrians were not into casinos and exotic dancers. At least, not in their backyard. If they had to travel to Munson, that was fine.

The parking lot of the bankrupted business was a hang for skate boarders and the generous green space was essentially a trash heap. Liv suggested they dig up the dead grass for not just their garden but start a community garden! They were able to win the hearts of the town council with their ambitious project by promising to pay for the trash removal. It was made very clear to Flynn and Liv that should a buyer for the building finally materialize the couple would be responsible to restore the green space to its previous condition.

But without the trash and the dead grass.

The next hurdle was to locate the gas and power lines. Fortunately, they were located on the other side of the building so the digging began in earnest. Initially, Liv did not want to use a gas-powered rototiller, because it clearly wasn't green, but as winter was setting in, they wanted to get something in the ground to enrich the soil. They rented a rototiller from the hardware store and also purchased seed. They went with wheat as the cover crop.

Water was the next issue. They had initially been using the outside tap on the old restaurant, but the town frowned on the use of water without paying for it. Liv bought a dozen rain barrels and positioned them under the down spouts of the abandoned business. She spoke extensively to the prospective community gardeners about mulching and handed out flyers about water conservation. After making financial compensations to the town of Huckleberry for the stealing of the water; Liv also paid for the installation of a water meter.

Liv had never worked so hard in her life and she loved it. Their garden project was up and running, their restaurant numbers looked good, and she couldn't remember the last time she had a migraine.

Now if she could only get this fat oaf to stop with the pesticide, her life would be perfect. Well, almost perfect. There was still that thing that happened this morning. She could not even think the words. It was that thing between her and Flynn that, if true, would end everything. Liv knew she'd have to deal with it soon, but not today; today there was lunch to serve!

***

Saffron giggled when Liv showed up a half an hour after lunch started. She could hear Flynn talking to her in that patronizing tone he always had.

"We only have the one meal to serve a day Liv. Do you think you can make it here on time tomorrow? Can you do that for me? Or is there something more important on your agenda? Can you check your calendar for me and let me know?"

"Give it a rest," Liv sighed, "You know damn well I was at the garden harvesting." She dumped the box full of beets and carrots on the floor. "Can you pick that up Flynn?" she said and sarcastically added, "Can you do that for me?"

Flynn did not give it a rest. "I am very disappointed in you Liv, I thought we were supposed to be a partnership. I don't see you holding up your end of the deal." He put his hand on her shoulder and was surprised how warm she felt. "Where's your work ethic Liv?" he asked.

"My work ethic? I financed the start-up costs to purchase and renovate this dive, I pay the bills, I do the gardening, I train the staff, I do the serving and the dishes, I even sweep the damn floor! What, pray tell, do you do Flynn?"

Gore in the *Garden*

Flynn continued in his same sanctimonious tone. "I do the menu planning and cooking Liv. Remember? We're a partnership."

Liv was not having a good day. She had a surprising phone call in the morning which left her feeling betrayed and powerless, then she had argued with the pesticide man with no results. Then Flynn humiliated her in front of that bit of fluff, Saffron. She felt impotent and lashed out with sarcasm.

"Oh, we're a partnership are we? You might want to mention that to your wife in the city."

Flynn dropped all the beets that he had just picked up. His whole persona changed from domineering boss to guilty schoolboy caught without having his homework done.

"Oops," he said.

With that one word Liv was completely deflated. All morning she had been wrestling with a couple of theories. She initially hoped it was a prank call from one of his sandwich delivery friends. Or it was his ex-wife just being nasty. Flynn had mentioned an ex-wife once or twice.

The woman had said, "Tell Flynn to drop this all natural crap and get home." When Liv had asked politely, "Who's calling please?" The woman said, "It's Misha, his wife. Lady, you should really get a handle on this restaurant. Flynn has been helping you out for months, surely you should have learned how to cook by now?"

Liv realized Flynn had been living a double life. His frequent trips to the city for organic spices and herbs that they didn't have time to grow; his mysterious phone calls he always took in another room of their apartment, that white line on his ring finger that never tanned all added up. He had played her big time.

Liv saw Saffron smirking behind Flynn. One problem at a time, Liv thought.

"Were you just on vacay this whole time?" she asked Flynn, "Was this your Peter Pan mid-life crisis?"

Flynn attempted to regain composure. "My wife and I were separated, and I saw you making such great strides in adopting a healthier lifestyle that I was attracted to you." Flynn started using expansive gestures to explain his point of view. "I thought, well, this is something Liv and I could do together! It would be so beautiful to just leave the city behind, get out of the rat race and embrace a vegan life!"

At this point Flynn smiled just as one of Liv's team members would do after they made what they thought was a successful pitch.

Liv had misread Saffron's smirk. Saffron had been the victim of a dirty rotten two timer, and she was smirking at Flynn's pathetic attempts to smooth things over. She walked up to Liv and with a new found confidence she asked Liv, "Are you buying any of this?"

"No, not really."

Still staring at Flynn, Saffron asked Liv, "It sounds like you bought everything to begin with. Everything in your name still?"

Liv turned and looked at Saffron with a new found interest; was there really a brain firing under those curls?

"Yes," Liv said slowly, "Everything is in my name still. I was just too busy to change things." She looked at Flynn. "Imagine that? Me with my poor work ethic, too busy to change the bank account and the restaurant title into joint names."

Flynn kept smiling. It had worked for him in the past so why change?

Saffron tapped Liv on the shoulder. "May I suggest three things, Boss?"

"Um, sure?"

"Keys, keys and address."

Liv was confused. She was trying not to punch Flynn in the nose.

Gore in the *Garden*

"What?" she demanded.

Saffron counted off on her fingers. "One, get the keys to the restaurant, two, get the keys to the apartment and three, get his mailing address and ship everything of his to his wife!"

Liv approached Flynn and put her arm around his shoulder. "Can you do something for me Flynn?"

He happily put his arm around her waist. "Of course Liv, but you know, the lunch rush is still on; they'll be needing their baked apple crunch soon."

Liv continued in a patronizing tone, "Could you give me your key ring? Could you do that for me Flynn?"

Flynn finally started to suspect that things were not going his way. As Liv stripped his key ring of the apartment key and the restaurant key, it started to hit home. He started to beg.

"I'm going to leave her, Liv. We just have to work out some custody issues with the kids."

"Kids?" Liv's eyes were as large as dinner plates. She grabbed a linen napkin and gave Flynn a pen.

"Write!" she demanded.

Saffron pulled on Liv's arm and said, "Find your center. Let the rage go. Be the better person." She then added, "I hope you don't mind I said that my Mom always tells me the same thing when I'm upset."

Liv started plating the dessert and showed Saffron the presentation included two mint leaves and three pumpkin seeds in a pretty flower.

After he had written down his mailing address, Flynn stood holding the pen.

Liv walked by him and pointed to the back door. "Oh you? You're fired. Out you go."

Flynn did a double take. "How am I supposed to get home? I don't even have a car!"

Just as the word 'oops' had done, the word 'home' cut Liv straight to the heart.

"Bus," she said as she again pointed to the door. She then loaded up two trays and she and Saffron went out to the dining room without a backwards glance.

And in the community garden, not too far away, Leon Pitre sank to his knees and fell face first in the dirt.

***

A couple of days later, Gracie stood in the lineup for Las Vegans. She wasn't a foodie, or a vegan, but she had heard good things about this strange little restaurant. She also had an interview with a prospective client scheduled.

A young woman, with the most gorgeous set of long auburn curls, was ushering patrons in the door. Her nametag said she was 'Saffron'. Even her voice was beautiful while she was counting.

"Eight, nine, ten, oh didn't see you there. Wow are you short! Eleven, twelve, thirteen…"

Gracie held up her hand, "I don't know if you should count me, I won't be eating. I'm here to see Liv Hayashi on a personal matter. I'm Gracie Noseworthy."

"Go right in and to the kitchen. She's expecting you. Now do I count you or not?"

The crowd yelled, "Don't count her!"

Saffron giggled. "Okay. Now what number was I at?"

Gracie said, "Twelve because you're not counting me. See you inside."

She walked inside and smiled. Six little tables were set up for four diners each. Gracie noticed a sign on the wall and smiled wider. "Do not move tables or chairs. Just sit with friends you haven't met yet."

Gore in the *Garden*

She walked in the kitchen and saw a tall woman popping what looked like meatloaf out of bread pans.

"You must be Liv," said Gracie extending her hand. "I know that isn't meatloaf, but it sure looks like it, and smells heavenly!"

"It's the cumin." Liv said. "You must be Gracie. Here, have a taste and tell me what you think. It's a new recipe for me and I'm a little nervous."

"Liv, this is to die for! Seriously. I can't place the basic ingredient though, what is it?"

"You're going to be surprised. Cooked brown lentils and sweet potatoes. Glad you liked it." Liv kept dishing up the plates. Saffron had finished her counting, closed the door; put up the sign that said "full; try again tomorrow" and was now serving.

"You've got a pretty busy operation here. When can we discuss why you called me?" Gracie asked.

"There'll be a break soon once we get these dishes out. I'll be right back."

Gracie stood in the kitchen peering out at the dining room. My goodness, she thought, I've hosted more people for dinner at my home! How can she possibly be making money? This must be more a labor of love than a viable business.

Gracie saw a brochure for the restaurant and began reading it. When she read the cover price, she revised her opinion.

"Twenty-five bucks a head? Wow. Maybe she is making money!"

"That I am!" said Liv. "I am considering opening for dinner, but I don't know. I'll have to look at the numbers and quite frankly, I'm tired of looking at the bottom line. I just want to enjoy life. That's one of the reasons I called you after reading your ad."

Gracie ran an ad in the local newspaper, just after the personal columns. Gracie's ad was just as, if not more, intriguing:

Shelley Dawn Siddall

"Did you do something bad, but can't quite remember? Did your neighbor do something bad, and you want to get the goods on them? Contact Gracie Noseworthy Investigations at 555-2368. I sniff out trouble!"

From the dining room, an acoustic guitar was being strummed. A male voice began singing an upbeat folk tune.

Gracie said, "Excuse me a minute," and peeked into the dining room. She had not seen a singer when she walked in.

"Look up," said Liv.

There, perched on a balcony that ran around the entire dining room was a young man with a guitar. He sang beautifully.

"I love seeing the look on people's faces when he starts singing. No one ever thinks to look up when they come in."

"Well it's a delightful surprise!" Gracie said as Liv put a plate of lentil loaf and potatoes in front of her.

"You eat, I'll talk," ordered Liv.

Gracie nodded as she dug into the lunch.

"A member of my community garden died a couple of days ago. His name was Leon Pitre. The thing is, I was having an argument with him shortly before he died about his use of pesticide. I was really steamed. When I left to come here, around 12:30, the last thing I said to him was, "I'm going to kill you if you keep this up." A lot of people were around, and everybody heard me. The police say he was murdered."

Gracie licked her fork. Despite having a good friend on the force, Detective Sergeant Ted Bailey, she didn't know Leon Pitre had died, but she did have a suspect. She needed to rule out Liv first though.

"How?" she asked.

"That's the thing. Someone stuck him with his pesticide spray gun." Liv blushed. "During the course of our very loud argument,

I may have suggested he put the spray gun somewhere extremely unpleasant."

Gracie grimaced. "Was that where it was found?"

"Heavens no! Ugh, that would have been gross. No, someone stuck it in his neck. I have an alibi, I was busy here, firing my so-called partner, but that's another story. The thing is, I'm afraid the police are going to blame me. All the gardeners who saw us arguing weren't sure of the time and the patrons dining didn't see me until later when I served dessert. I've already had a policeman come to the apartment and interview me. I think his name was Dave something or other. I have his card in my purse. He did not believe anything I said."

"It wasn't Dave Shufeldt was it?"

"Yes! That was the name. Why, do you know him?"

Gracie scraped the last of her meal off the plate and ate it. "Good to the last bite. Dave is a good friend of mine. He and his wife Pauline are on the same bowling team with me. They both have a quirky sense of humor. Dave likes to play bad cop. He thinks it unsettles the suspect."

"It did; it still does. Got to go; dessert is up next."

Liv and her assistant began unloading ramekins from the fridge onto trays.

Saffron said excitedly, "It's avocado chocolate mousse!"

While they were busy serving the twenty-four diners, Gracie phoned Ted.

"What's this about Leon Pitre being murdered?" she asked.

"And hello to you too Gracie. Do you have Liv Hayashi as a new client?"

"Yes indeedy. And I must say she is most distraught about her interview the other night. You'll have to tell Dave his bad cop routine finally worked. She's rattled. So what do you think, did she do it?"

Shelley Dawn Siddall

"You know time of death isn't an exact science. I think she could have, but the trouble is, Pitre's death went unnoticed for a while." Ted then added facetiously, "You may not have known this but Pitre had quite the reputation as the town drunk."

Gracie wondered if there was any dessert left in the fridge. Would it be rude if she looked?

"Were you at the same garden party I was Ted? Mr. Pitre was pickled and pretty sure his wife was trying to kill him. Why is Liv on the hook?"

"Rest assured, Gracie, we are looking at his wife, but she wasn't there."

"Wait, Liv said that a whole lot of people heard and saw their argument. How did no one notice a murder taking place under their very noses?" Gracie added as she opened the fridge door, "Oh good! There are more ramekins!"

"People saw Pitre laying on the ground and they just figured he was sleeping it off. But the thing was, he sobered up a few weeks ago according to Julia Smith, his neighbor. Poor little thing, she was heartbroken when she heard the news.

"Anyhow, Liv Hayashi may have done a stealth like ninja move, stabbed him in the neck and no one saw him drop. The body has to be shipped to Munson for the autopsy, but the Coroner suggested that he could have been overcome by the pesticide fumes and stabbed later. We won't know until the autopsy results and the tox screen comes in. Apparently, Pitre was using some toxic liquid that he had in the back of his garage for years. Pauline checked it out on-line and said it had been banned for years."

"So who discovered the body?" Gracie asked. She had helped herself to the mousse. It was fabulous.

"Unfortunately, it was his wife. She had brought him his lunch and found him with the gun thing sticking out of his neck."

Gore in the *Garden*

Gracie stopped eating. "His wife? Oh no, Liv Hayashi didn't do this. His wifey-poo should jump to the top of your list!" She could hear Liv and Saffron returning. "Explain later," she said and hung up.

"Sorry for the wait," Liv said, "But we always go round to the tables and get payment for the meal when we serve dessert. That way, people can relax and enjoy the music."

"The guitar player is my boyfriend," Saffron said proudly. "He works at Billy's Burgers in Munson. I was going to go work there, but with you know who gone, I like it here."

Liv smiled. "It was Saffron who suggested we get Nate to play at lunch. We don't pay him, but he can sell his music."

"He has a sign showing where you can download his music. Plus, Liv lets me air drop a free sample to their phone if the customers want it."

"And speaking of free samples, here is my twenty for this excellent meal. You'll notice I helped myself to dessert." Gracie advised. "As far as your concern about the incident at the Community Garden…"

Liv interrupted. "Don't worry, I told Saffron all about what the police suspect."

"In that case, I suspect that you will be dropped as a suspect in about twenty-four hours or less. I can't say much more, but I will phone you as soon as you are off the possible murderer list."

Gracie turned to Saffron. "My boyfriend is a Detective on the Huckleberry Police Force." She turned back to Liv, "That's how I know Dave Shufeldt; my boyfriend is his boss."

Saffron squealed and punched Liv in the arm. "The girl has connections! You're safe!"

***

Gracie's phone had been beeping non-stop with text messages from Ted. She hopped in her car and called him back.

"I've got you on speaker on the car phone; what's up?"

"Why is Evelyn Pitre a suspect? What do you know that I don't?"

"Small reminder Ted; I'm your girlfriend, not a criminal to be grilled. But, if I were a fish, I would prefer to be grilled rather than baked. It would all be over much sooner."

"Gracie my dear, I am sorry for my outburst, but time is of the essence. At the garden party for death, Pitre did accuse his wife, but we have her at home helping her neighbor with some fountain thing. Please tell me your theory of the crime. Also, are you going home? I can meet you there."

Gracie turned towards home. She had wanted to talk to Jasmine at the hospice, but that could wait. After all, Petra wouldn't complain.

"I have it on good authority that Mrs. Pitre wanted to kill Mr. Pitre long before he announced it. I have a signed letter to that effect; but again, it's not direct evidence, just hearsay. My theory is based on the singular oddity of Mrs. Pitre bringing lunch to Mr. Pitre. I think she walked up to him, saw him on the ground and just picked up the spray gun and stabbed him. Then she waited until he bled out and then called the cops."

Gracie heard Ted say 'good theory' just as she turned into her driveway.

"At home Ted; see you soon."

***

About two weeks later, Ted and Gracie were numbers seven and eight at Las Vegans. Once they sat down, Gracie asked Ted, "What is it with us and numbers?"

Gore in the *Garden*

"And death," he said.

"So, no fingerprints on the pesticide thingy, but you did find some that nailed her. Where?"

"She had wiped the gun clean but forgot that she had put her hand on the ledge Pitre built around his raised garden bed."

Gracie hadn't been to the community garden and hadn't seen his little garden, but she was pretty sure you couldn't get fingerprints off wood. She told Ted so.

"You're right, but Pitre had decided to jazz up his little corner of paradise by gluing a very nice tile on his ledge." Ted leaned forward and raised one bushy eyebrow. "A glass tile. Lifting her fingerprints from the glass tile was easy-peasy."

The couple was seated and eagerly looked to the chalk board for today's lunch.

"Oh, look who's here," Gracie whispered to Ted, "It's Conrad and Julia. Nice."

Ted added with a grin, "Ah young love! I imagine they're not talking about death and murder. Look at the menu! Roasted Portobello Mushroom Tacos with Creamy Carrot Slaw. This is going to be fabulous!"

***

Conrad and Julia were talking about death. This was their first official date even though both of them knew Julia was still married.

Julia's speech at the garden party had endeared her to Conrad and vice versa. Julia was explaining about Brett, about his truck and how she was pretty sure he was dead. She was also missing Mr. Pitre. She even missed his singing.

In the kitchen, Saffron was happy. Liv had finally let her buy some spring loaded mouse traps which Saffron had baited with peanut butter. There was a loud snap. Saffron was pretty sure that mouse was dead; she hoped she heard a lot more snaps before the week was out. No sooner had she thought that when another snap sounded. It was weirdly satisfying.

Gore in the *Garden*

Thyme to Die

"Did she go back to that Chef blue place in France?"

"I think what you mean is Le Cordon Bleu in Paris France. Imagine, going all that way to learn how to cook!"

"For twenty bucks, I could have showed her how to make macaroni and cheese."

Gales of laughter rang out.

Myron Flores heard these comments as he sat in the Town Hall. He knew who they were talking about, Mrs. Lily Davis, his cold fish of a neighbor. Lily and Mark had moved into the house directly across from Myron about three years before. Mark was some sort of computer geek and Lily did something in computers as well.

The first thing they did when they moved in was to literally rip off their front door. They took the door off the hinges and threw it on the grass beside their steps. Mark watched with fascination and his binoculars from one of his upstairs bedrooms.

Myron assumed that they had to take the door off to move big pieces of furniture in, but they moved in delicate little things that Myron would squash in a minute if he ever sat on one. Myron didn't know why the Davis' had hired movers; the couple micromanaged the carrying of every stick of furniture and more often than not, ended up ordering the movers to put the items down.

Myron could hear all this with a boom microphone he happened to have pointed in the direction of the red brick house across the road.

"Town Meeting will now come to order, Mayor Hazel Froment presiding."

Myron stopped his wool gathering and got out his pen and paper to take notes even though he had a mini-recorder in his jacket pocket. Sometimes the recorder didn't pick up everything.

Hazel Froment walked up to the podium and began her well attended speech.

"As most of you know, Munson has been wanting to open negotiations to expand into Huckleberry…"

"Take it over, more like it," someone yelled from the audience.

"And build a massive condo complex with its own shopping mall and car dealership! Just what you want to see when you're paddle-boarding on Wasabi Lake!"

Mayor Froment ignored these comments and continued, "It does seem rather forceful doesn't it? Hence this meeting. The big city of Munson has brought forth documents that purport to show ownership of land in East Huckleberry should the current owner decease or decide to sell. In particular, the five acre parcels that front Jubilee Road and extend all the way to Wasabi Lake.

"As we know, there is no access to Wasabi Lake except on the Munson side, as all the land on the Huckleberry side is privately owned and has been for generations. The Munson documents claim that as of this year, ownership changes. For example, now that Mr. Walters has died, his land reverts to the city of Munson. We also have a secondary issue; Miss Barbara Shires and Mr. Barry Frederickson have listed their respective properties for sale. It was a title search that triggered someone in Munson to notify the City Fathers. They in turn claim that, as of this year, once the land is put up for sale, they are entitled to pay the current owner what Munson deems as a fair market value and take over the land.

"Rip-off Artists! Fair market value my eye!"

"What about Mr. Walter's daughter? Doesn't she inherit?"

The Mayor stared into the audience. "Mrs. Gracie Noseworthy and Miss Barbara Shire if you could contain yourselves and keep your comments and questions until the end of the session, it will be appreciated."

She then went on and on about the wording of an old document and the cost of a current legal interpretation.

Myron zoned out and started to think about Lily Davis again. He had gone over and introduced himself after he had given them some time to settle in. He brought a lovely lemon pound cake he had bought at the bakery. Lily had taken the cake from him and almost immediately, pretended to drop it.

"What is this? Lead pound cake?"

Both Lily and Mark had laughed. Myron had not.

Lily made it worse by adding, "Well, we can always use it as a door stop."

Myron had admired their new door from across the road. It had gone in the same day they moved in. A beautiful beet red door with nearly a full glass pane that had a striking willow design etched in. Myron looked at the door as Lily dropped the cake in front of it.

She. Dropped. His. Cake.

Mark rushed in and scooped up the cake saying, "Lily, if this gets squished by the door it's going to be a bear to clean off!"

Mark handed the cake back to Myron.

"Thanks, but no thanks," said Lily and shut the door.

It was then Myron decided to kill them. But it wasn't time yet. He had to gather more intel.

Myron wasn't the only one in the audience whose thoughts drifted. Shane Mitchell was thinking about his recent deal with the devil.

"She would be the Mayor," he thought despondently. Shane had never been owned by anyone; sure he had pretended to be, but he could always chose when to walk out. And he usually walked out with a fair bit of cash.

This time he was hooped. He liked where he was living a bit too much and so he put up with the humiliating requirements to live in Hazel's carriage house.

Before the meeting, she had introduced him as her new pool boy. Him! A fifty-five year old gentleman with the physique of an Adonis!

Shane sighed. Maybe he was just a pool boy now.

***

"I think we might have a chance with the phrase 'a preponderance of opinion'," Gracie said to Trudy-Faye during the coffee-break.

"I'm sorry Gracie, I just don't see the issue. Why does anyone want to stand in the way of progress?"

"You're a Realtor; of course you're wanting progress for the good of everyone in Huckleberry. It has nothing to do with the commissions you'll make if you and William move to Munson and sell condos."

Trudy-Faye choked on her Nanaimo bar.

"Gracie Noseworthy you are just too smart for your own good," she retorted and walked away.

Gracie didn't feel too smart. There was something she was missing about this whole 'old document' business. She looked over at the chairs in front of the podium. Only two were occupied. Barb

Gore in the *Garden*

Shire and Barry Frederickson were deep in discussion. Barry would shrug occasionally and pat Barb's back consolingly. Barb continually fanned herself and looked on the verge of tears.

"This seems a bit more serious than trying to sell their properties for a good price," Gracie thought, "Maybe I'll just wander over and see what's going on."

Her plan was interrupted by a portly man holding an uneaten donut.

"You're that Gracie from the ad in the paper, aren't you? I have an interesting theory if you want to hear it."

Gracie ran an ad in the local paper which read:

"Did you do something bad, but can't quite remember? Did your neighbor do something bad, and you want to get the goods on them? Contact Gracie Noseworthy Investigations at 555-2368. I sniff out trouble!"

"Yes I am and yes I do; I just need to know your name first," said Gracie, eyeing the donut with some interest.

"Myron Flores. I live over in the 'berries."

The 'berries referred to one of the oldest subdivisions in Huckleberry. All the streets were named after berries. Myron had lived on Thimbleberry Street his entire life.

Gracie shook his hand. "Nice area; I love all those Victorian style homes. Well, once they're updated. Call me materialistic, but I love having an ensuite and a thermal paned windows! What did you want to discuss?"

Myron liked this lady; she was easy on the eyes. She had a warm, but more importantly, firm handshake. His Dad always said you can judge a person by the strength of their handshake and Dad was usually right about everything.

"Firstly, you're on the wrong track with the word preponderance. That word comes from the Latin and has been around for hundreds of years; so that wouldn't prove the document a fake," Myron explained.

"I did not know that. Okay; what's your theory?"

"I think this old document was recently faked by those who will gain financially, but not by this proposed condo development. The zoning will not pass, even in Munson."

Gracie narrowed her eyes for two reasons. Myron seemed to be a man who knew a little about a lot of things. The second reason? He still had not taken a bite.

"Are you going to eat that donut, or what?" Gracie asked with a grin.

Myron blushed. "It's a new weight loss technique I'm trying. You can have anything you want, but you just can't eat it. You hold the item you want, and psychologically it stops the craving."

"Is it working?"

Myron handed Gracie the donut and continued with his other theory. "I think the ulterior motive is to build up Wasabi Lake into a destination resort area."

"Interesting," Gracie said between bites. "What has led you to this particular conclusion?"

Myron looked around the town hall and put his finger on the side of his nose.

"The walls have ears, you know."

Gracie polished off the donut and was licking her fingers. "No, I don't think so. Please just tell me your reasons." Myron suddenly looked incredibly sad, so she reconsidered. "If you would feel more comfortable, we can step outside and discuss this."

Once outside, Myron looked pleased and noticeably relaxed.

"I'm currently unemployed, medical leave you know, but I used to work in the City of Munson as one of the cashiers. Like any employee considered by management as working in a menial job, I was invisible." Myron smiled. "Yes, a man of my size was invisible.

Gore in the *Garden*

When I wasn't at the wicket, I was at a desk located by the Zoning Commissioner's office. I heard things."

Gracie nodded and murmured, "I can imagine." She still didn't know if Myron had anything worthwhile, but it was an intriguing theory. She wondered though, what he expected her to do with the information? She put a pin in that thought and heard him out.

"So, I could hear the Commissioner on his phone and one day I heard him say, "Oh that will never pass, it's just a red herring to get the Lake Resort and Casino through. Just think if we can pull this off we'll have the whole lake. We could build three or four more hotel resorts. We could be the next Atlantic City, but you know, on a lake. And smaller."

If Gracie had any of the donut left, she would have choked like Trudy-Faye. This was unbelievable if it were true!

"Well, you could knock me down with a feather! What is it you want me to do?" she asked.

"I want to hire you to figure out who is behind this. I think that anyone who has been quietly buying up old cabins with lake frontage would be a good place to start. Once we find out who is attempting to profit from zoning changes, we can squash this takeover of Huckleberry like a bug!" Myron dug his wallet out of his jeans and pulled out a hundred dollar bill.

"My down payment," he said.

Gracie accepted the money. "Did you work with anyone called Anita Ellis?"

"Also known as the former murderer, Mrs. Frederickson? No, why do you ask?"

"Just a possible thread I might pick at. Should I mail you the receipt?"

"Could you come by and meet my Dad? He has never met a celebrity before, and he would love to meet you. Here's my address and number."

Gracie agreed and entered the information in her phone. She then informally approached the Mayor as she had missed the question and answer period of the emergency meeting.

"Hazel don't make any decisions or agreements yet. I've got something I've got to look into with Ted. I think we're going undercover!"

***

"I knew it, I knew it, I knew it," Trudy-Faye said smugly. "I knew you two were going to end up together! But you could have knocked me over with a feather, when you said you wanted to live in Munson on Lake Wasabi!" She poked Gracie in the ribs.

Ted and Gracie continued to smile. It was torturous going around to see different properties for sale with the boisterous Trudy-Faye, but Ted was just as invested as Gracie in keeping Huckleberry a small town. Their crime rate was already off the charts and a huge influx of tourists, even if it was city adjacent, would not help.

"Of course I'll have to split my commission with the local realtor, but still it will be a nice amount. Now, can we give your budget a nudge?" Trudy-Faye was beyond jubilant. Being busy helped her forget some truths she was coming to grips with.

Ted and Gracie looked at one another. Trudy-Faye was treating them like a pair of teenage newlyweds, so Ted blinked his eyes rapidly, lifted one shoulder and slapped his hand against his chin. "It's just all too exciting," he fake squealed.

Gracie snorted with laughter.

"We really want a lot of lake frontage with whatever property we buy, so we may be able to bump up our budget," Ted said in his normal voice.

Gore in the *Garden*

Trudy-Faye clapped her hands. "Oh goodie! Now, there isn't that much to choose from; there has been a recent rash of sales, but I did find this little gem. It literally came on the market today. Mind the stairs, you can install new ones to suit your taste."

Despite the warning, Ted put his foot through the top stair as Gracie wisely walked down to the cabin in the foliage beside the three stairs.

Trudy-Faye continued to gush, "Really, the whole thing should be torn down, but you could hole up here while building your new place. You've got over two hundred feet of lake frontage. Of course, you might want to consider rebuilding the dock."

Gracie pointed to the water. "You mean the floating pile of rotting debris? Yes, we would definitely consider building a new dock. Now you said there were a lot of sales in the area. Would we get new neighbors right away? I wonder if we could coordinate the delivery of lumber?"

Trudy-Faye looked thoughtful. "Can't speak to that, Gracie and Ted, but it seems a cost-cutting measure. But yes, you will have new neighbors. In fact, all the waterfront on either side of this gem was snapped up by the same purchaser. This cabin hadn't come on the market yet otherwise I'm sure he would have bought it too. Now, let's go in the cabin."

Ted stepped very carefully on each tread of the steps up to the front door. The steps held and he scooted inside followed by the two women.

"Who bought all this surrounding area then?" asked Gracie.

Trudy-Faye rocked her head back and forth. "Well, I really shouldn't say, but you're going to be neighbors, so you'll find out soon enough. It was Hizzoner, the Mayor of Munson, Mr. Orvin Metcalfe!"

"I'm sure glad no one is in the habit of carrying feathers, or that would be the second time today I would have been easily knocked over," Gracie said sotto voce to Ted.

"Well, that's pretty much all we need to know," Gracie said in a louder voice.

Trudy-Faye was dismayed. "Oh no, this is the best part of showing a property. I love hearing the prospective home owner talk about where they are going to place their furniture and watching them measure and look out the windows at the view! And bicker; I do love me a good argument!" She leaned forward and crooked her finger towards Gracie and Ted. "It's mostly about two sinks in the bathroom and paint colors. The women all want to rip out the bathroom and the men, well, they want a workshop, but surprisingly, they do have strong feelings about the paint color."

Ted had a dry sense of humor and an excellent dead pan delivery of a line. He looked at the tongue and groove pine paneling that covered every square inch of the cabin. "I think the paint color is fine," he said.

"Oh no Ted," Trudy-Faye corrected, "This is paneling. It isn't painted at all."

"I see. Amazing. What color would you call this? I'd like to paint the station house this color."

Trudy-Faye wasn't entirely sure if he was serious, but she went on to the next point on her list. "Now, I'm going to step outside and let you just live in the space for a little while." She carefully made her way outside and started returning messages.

As much as Gracie wanted to make several phone calls, she started to seriously consider a course of action that might make all the difference to the secret resort destination plan.

"Ted, I think I should buy this. You know me, I not much for travelling. This place, once I re-build, would be an excellent weekend retreat for me and the cats."

Gore in the *Garden*

"Gracie, what about me? Do you think I could rent a room? Or live in the garage? Wait. There isn't one."

"Oh, I'm sure the cats won't mind if you come along. I am serious about buying this Ted. What if we can't prove that Orvin Metcalfe has this master plan? Maybe if I do buy this property, it will be the fly in the ointment."

Ted smiled. "Now I would have said 'the screw in the works' but I see your point. This property would curtail the change in zoning, one would hope. But maybe they would just build the casino etcetera on either side of you and use a zip line to get from one side to the other. "

Gracie looked up and watched several wasps squeeze through a hole in one of the boards in the ceiling. That's going to be an issue, she thought and made a note on her phone to purchase several epi-pens.

"I hope I'm not going to be branded a traitor to the Huckleberry township; but I'm going to buy this place."

She walked over to Ted and put her arm around his. "I did hear the subtext when you said, 'what about me'. Do we want to do this jointly? I'm game, but my only concern is that I have way more money than you and if I finance most of this project, you won't feel like it's your place."

"Don't worry Gracie, I have buckets of money."

"You do? Since when?"

"Grandma, Father, Step-Father, inheritance, stock market, blah blah blah. I'm loaded."

"Awesome! Let's do this thing!"

Ted frowned. "You don't have any ear plugs do you? Trudy-Faye's shrieking is going to be worse than any police siren."

***

Shelley Dawn Siddall

Myron had watched the renovations taking place at the Davis home over the months and years. Beside immediately replacing their front door, they had cut down the beautiful old lilac trees in the front yard.

This was almost blasphemous in Myron's mind. He had carefully helped the previous owner shape those trees. Initially they cut out all the dead wood and new shoots. Eventually the two trees formed a heart shape. Each fall, Myron would get his Dad's ladder and cut off all the old blooms. Each spring, he would rub off the new buds from the inside of the heart. Myron was very proud of those lilacs and when they bloomed, he always left his bedroom window open. The fragrance soothed him and reminded him that at least he had done one right thing in his life.

Lily and Mark Davis hired men to come and grind out the stumps so there was no hope that the lilacs would grow back. The sound the machines made burned into Myron's brain. He knew it was silly, but he felt like the lilacs were screaming.

Myron carefully kept track of all these heresies and promised that, at the proper time, his neighbors would die.

His binoculars could only show him so much, so he relied on his boom microphone. He had considered buying a drone and spying that way, but the learning curve would be too steep. According to the conversations he overheard, they were going to redo nearly every room in the house.

At some point though, early in the renovation extravaganza, Lily decided that she couldn't live in a construction zone so she would go to France and take cooking lessons. A week or two after she left, Mark came over and knocked on the door of the Flores home.

Mark was a changed man without Lily around. He fell all over himself apologizing for the lemon pound cake incident. He invited Myron to come over, anytime to view the changes.

Gore in the *Garden*

If Myron had the ability, he would have jumped up and clicked his heels. He went over to Mark's place, as he now called it, nearly every day. Myron bought himself a hardhat and steel toed shoes because he was in a construction zone. Mark said he didn't need to but agreed it was a good idea to be on the safe side.

Once all the rooms in the house had been done, Mark started working on the outside. The former owners had two large greenhouses and thus had vegetables year round and were the first to put out hanging flower baskets stuffed with beauties they had grown from seed.

Oddly enough, when Mark dismantled the greenhouses and the many raised gardens, Myron didn't want to kill him. Mark decided they needed a large patio area so they could have guests like the Flores family, for meals al fresco on warm summer evenings. Myron thought that was a reasonable idea. When Mark discussed placing pavement stones for a walkway, Myron suggested planting woolly thyme in between.

Mark was over the moon. He hugged Myron many times that day and they went to the nursery together to pick out the plants. The thyme grew quickly, and the walkway was a treat to look at. Myron even helped Mark trim the thyme every week, so it didn't look too unruly or takeover.

Then, after sixteen months away at the Cordon Bleu in Paris France, Lily came home in December. She had supervised the redo of the kitchen and the butler's pantry via Skype, but when she saw it in person, she was uncharacteristically effusive with praise to Mark.

Myron heard it all. He also heard her dictating to Mark that his tubby buddy Myron won't be coming over anymore. Myron did not fit with the theme of the house nor did he go with the brand of people that Lily wanted them to associate with.

Shelley Dawn Siddall

Myron had been lonely most of his life, but now he experienced a new kind of loneliness. One that sunk him to new depths of depression. To have a friendship, finally and then to have it ripped away; well, somebody had to pay.

Of course, it was going to be Lily. But only at the right time. You couldn't rush a thing like this, Myron knew.

The only thing that brought Myron comfort during this dark time in his life, was the increasing friction at the Davis household. As spring approached, and their second year of living across the road from Myron, Lily discovered the walkway that Mark had not consulted her on. She was incensed. She wanted a Terrazzo tiled walkway, just like the one in Hollywood with all the stars on it, to lead to the patio area. When Lily found out that the thyme had to be trimmed weekly, she flipped and bawled Mark out.

It was Mark's turn to flip. He told Lily that they were going to finish landscaping the backyard the way he wanted it and that's the way it was going to be!

She had never been talked to that way by anybody, let alone Mark. She spluttered and stuttered and finally came up with a response.

"You can fill the damn thing up with rocks, for all I care," she said.

So Mark did. For nearly two years he had been fighting a losing battle with the blackberry bushes along the lot line at the back of his property. Despite his best efforts, they continued to creep ever closer to his beautiful patio. So after ripping them out, yet again, he built an eight foot high retaining wall the entire width of his property. He ordered the aggregate and rented a stone slinger complete with operator.

Unbeknownst to Lily, the two friends chatted via computer during the six months she was back. Myron had broached a certain subject with Mark during one of their clandestine computer chats.

Gore in the *Garden*

He suggested a course of action and Mark simply said, "I'll sign off on this project."

On the day the machine was due to arrive, Myron was ready. It was time. He almost ran over to Mark's place. Almost. Even though he had lost forty pounds when he was chumming with Mark, in the six months Lily had been back, Myron's weight had returned. Another thing Lily had to die for.

Lily yelled for Mark when she opened the door and saw Myron standing there. Myron was not wearing his hardhat and steel toed shoes and was quite perturbed about that, but he didn't let it show. Lily kept screaming for Mark to come and talk to his tubby friend, but Mark didn't answer.

"I just want to take before and after shots of the backyard." Myron showed Lily his phone and asked her if he should just keep ringing the bell until Mark showed up. Reluctantly, Lily escorted Myron to the backyard and stayed with him because people of Myron's sort might attempt to steal things.

Myron needed a ladder. With much effort, he managed to prop the ladder up against the wall. Unfortunately, he couldn't climb the ladder. But Lily didn't realize that at first. Myron started to climb but as soon as his foot touched the first rung, he said he felt faint. He took his foot off. He put it back on. Felt faint again. Took his foot off.

Of course Lily was exasperated beyond belief.

"You little turd, hand me your phone and I'll take the damn picture," she said.

Myron handed her a cheap phone he had purchased for the occasion.

Lily climbed part way up the later. Myron quietly told himself, it's not time; don't rush it.

"Well now I can't see anything because this damn ladder is in the way," Lily complained. She leaned out to the side of the ladder and started looking for the camera icon on the phone.

Now was the time. Myron wedged himself under the ladder and with a herculean effort, he stood up, lifting the end of the ladder. It began to pivot on the wall and Lily began cursing in earnest.

Myron pushed his arms up with all his might. He thought for a moment that Lily was going to jump off, but just in time, Mark stood and reached up from the other side and pulled the ladder and Lily down.

Myron heard a couple of pops, then the scrape as Mark leaned the ladder against his side of the retaining wall. Mark climbed up, stood on the wall, and took a picture. Then he lifted the ladder over and climbed back down to where Myron waited.

"Done and dusted," Mark said as he put the handgun back in his pocket. "I put an old tarp over her just in case the machine operator looks over the edge."

"Good idea. Can you send me an email of those pictures?"

Mark didn't want to disappoint his buddy, but he suggested a different way to send the images. "I think I better print them on my home computer and then you can pick them up tomorrow."

"And we'll probably need to trim the thyme too."

The two friends watched in awe as the stone slinger operator expertly maneuvered the conveyor to the edge of the wall. The operator was going to peer over, but Myron asked, "What are you looking for?"

"Just want to make sure no animals went in there! We don't want to hurt any neighborhood cats."

We just want to bury one, thought Myron.

Even though he was assured by Mark, the operator took a quick glance, but didn't notice the tarp up against the foundation of the retaining wall. He started his machine.

Gore in the *Garden*

The neighbors who thought they heard something like a car backfiring earlier, came out to see what was going on. As they heard the rumble of the machine and the noise of stones being thrown they convinced themselves that this was the noise the machine made when it started up. In no time at all, Mark's blackberry problem was solved. Permanently.

That was last year. Last winter, Myron and Mark had rebuilt a greenhouse. Now, at Mark's place a plethora of pots graced the rock bed, all overflowing with flowers. Myron had lost fifty pounds and had gained a lot of confidence. Tons of it, in fact.

He even got the courage to go to the Doctor about his issues. The Doctor referred him to a specialist who told him he needed to take a medical leave. Myron began going out in public more and started to take an interest in city politics. He still couldn't believe that just that day he went to a town meeting where he actually talked to Gracie Noseworthy and hired her!

His Dad was really proud of Myron. He hadn't told Mark yet.

***

Gracie was thinking over a rum and coke at her house. She couldn't put her finger on it, but something was wrong.

Someone, during the course of the day had body language that was out of sync with their surroundings. Gracie pulled at her memory threads; it was as a result of a conversation she overheard, but she couldn't get any further.

It wasn't Ted, he was always forthright with her. Other than not sharing that he had buckets of money, he was an open book. Or was he? No; it wasn't Ted. What about Trudy-Faye? Well, she was an open book too. Clearly her over-jubilant manner was her compensating for the death of her son.

Gracie shuddered involuntarily. I really hope she doesn't ask me to investigate his death further, she thought. I've got to keep Petra's secret. It wasn't Hazel or her sulky pool boy. What about Myron Flores? He had given them a lot of good information as it turned out.

But what was it about him that was off? She thought back to when he first caught her attention. Apropos of nothing, he was suddenly grinning before the meeting even started. Shortly afterwards the two women laughed about somebody taking a cooking course.

That was it! Myron was grinning before the sarcastic comment about the macaroni and cheese was made. Now what did that woman say to begin with? 'Did she go back to…' Sounds like another missing woman..

Gracie polished off her drink. She was going to check into her latest client Myron. Good thing she had promised to meet his Dad. She could beard the lion in his den.

Later that night, Myron received a phone call from Mark.

"What do you mean you hired Gracie Noseworthy? She's a busybody. Her name is mentioned in the papers as helping the police to solve murders. We don't need her sniffing around!"

Myron was taken aback. Mark had never talked to him like that. Mark was changing of late. He was talking a lot more about some woman he had met called Jasmine.

"Gracie is just as sweet as pie. I hired her about this Munson thing. Don't worry Mark, I've got it all under control."

The two friends chatted about more pleasant things, the venting system in the greenhouse, the proper method to prune roses and other such things. Both felt much better at the end of the call.

Still, Myron sat thinking after he hung up. He opened and closed the special scissors he bought when he started going over to Mark's to trim the thyme. Perhaps he should reconsider his friendship with Mark. Time would tell.

Shelley Dawn Siddall

Don't Get Up On The Wrong Side Of The Bed!

Conrad really liked Julia. She reminded him of a beautiful dream that misted away when you woke. He could never quite figure out what he liked about her; was it simply that she was the first young woman that had been nice to him since he got out of prison?

Or was it because she was so pretty and seemed so innocent? And yet, he also admired her depth. When she revealed part of her story at the garden party for death, he felt himself tear up. He could identify with depression and suicidal ideation.

Conrad needed someone to talk to. He had called on Gracie Noseworthy before and she had helped him greatly; she even let him stay in her spare bedroom. Even though he knew her number off by heart, he got his wallet out and carefully unfolded the clipping that was so precious to him. It read:

"Did you do something bad, but can't quite remember? Did your neighbor do something bad, and you want to get the goods on them? Contact Gracie Noseworthy Investigations at 555-2368. I sniff out trouble!"

Gore in the *Garden*

It was this little clipping that changed Conrad's entire life. Yes, he would phone Gracie; she would know what to do.

***

Julia woke up with such a keen sense of happiness, she started to sing one of the late Mr. Pitre's favorite songs.

"One hundred bottles of beer on the wall, a hundred bottles of beer! Take one down, pass it around, ninety-nine bottles of beer on the wall!"

She jumped out of bed, threw on a cotton dress and ran to the backyard to see her garden. It had grown considerably since Brett; her late husband had disappeared some months before. She turned on the fountain she had installed and watched as the water flowed down the sculpture from the tap beside a little girl to where a little boy was washing a dog in a bucket.

She had named all three figures in the sweet tableau.

"Good morning Della, and Tom and Bam-Bam! How are you all this morning?" Fortunately, she wasn't expecting them to answer.

Julia then walked to the fence and dead-headed the petunias growing out of brightly colored gumboots she had nailed to the fence. Out of the corner of her eye she could see the dozens of whirly-gigs twirling in the slight breeze. Notwithstanding the profusion of flowers, Julia had several barren spots in her backyard, all carefully prepared for the remaining projects on her list.

Her thrift store magazines had talked about a moonlight garden. That was going to be thrilling! She had purchased several allium bulbs; but still had not decided on which flowers were going to accompany them. She wanted ones that had not only highly reflective petals, but interesting shapes in silhouette. Because she was unsure, she put that project on hold.

Without even eating breakfast, she started in on her current project. It was hard work but was going to be fantastic when it was done! It was a riot of color already. Yesterday, she had gone to a tire store and scrounged around in their cast off pile, gathered a dozen tires of varying sizes and brought them home and washed them. She was now painting them; each had a distinctive color. Steadily mauve, lime green, butter yellow, turquoise, and forest green tires appeared. Julia went on to paint a red tire, a white tire and a pink one. She liked the yellow and turquoise so much she painted another two tires those colors.

It was a long morning, so she left the last two tires unpainted and went in her home for breakfast.

"Well, that morning flew by!" she said, "It's already 11:30. I may as well have tacos for brunch."

She checked her phone and noticed that Conrad had phoned several times. Did they have an appointment to do something? Julia didn't think so. She'd call him back after she had eaten. Another thought occurred to her; maybe he could help her arrange the tires in a pyramid against the back fence?

Not that she really needed his help. She had done all of the other work herself, with the exception of the underground irrigation. The late Mr. Pitre, bless his drunken heart, had helped her with that.

And of course, she was ever so grateful he had killed her husband and buried him in her front yard.

Julia added some hot salsa and guacamole to her tacos. It was a shame Mr. Pitre died. She had grown accustomed to walking with him the short distance around the fountain in her front yard to his home when he stumbled homewards from the pub on the weekends. Perhaps she should get a dog after all; she read that they enjoy regular walks.

***

Gracie gave Conrad a huge hug when she greeted him on her door step.

"My goodness me, it's been ages! I hear good things about you. Please come in! Ever since I picked up the phone and said your name, the kitties have been talking up a storm. They miss you terribly!"

On cue, Zoey and Frank ran up to Conrad, mewing and curling around his legs.

"Why hello there cutie-pies! How are you? How have you been? I've missed you too."

Conrad spent some time frolicking with the cats while Gracie got out a new file folder just in case he had another job for her.

"It's not really a job, more of a conversation I need. I'll gladly pay your regular fee," Conrad began.

"Oh no, let's just see how things go, before any money changes hands. Is this about Julia?" Gracie asked.

Conrad raised his eyebrows. "Now how did you get there?"

"I saw you two at the garden party and then at Las Vegans plus you keep checking your phone. I'm guessing your waiting for a text from Julia. I was wondering though, is this a little soon for you? After all, your Mom recently died, and I didn't know if you have fully processed that event."

Conrad nodded. "You see, I haven't got a sponsor since I came out of prison. I've been going to the meetings and I've been staying sober, but I haven't really clicked with anybody. Even though I have been sober for three years, I still need to work on my life skills."

"So you'd like to talk things over with me while your sponsor is 'in absentia' shall we say?"

Conrad grinned. "Nice legalese, Gracie. Yes. I'd like you to be my 'amicus curiae'."

"And what is the case before the court?"

"Several issues." Conrad again looked serious.

Zoey was having none of it and jumped in his lap. No friend of Zoey Noseworthy was going to feel down hearted. She would cheer him up! And if he also happened to be an excellent scratcher of necks, so be it. She climbed up his chest and began nuzzling his chin with the occasional head butt.

Gracie smiled. "Guess she decided you needed some extra loving. Please, go on."

"My reputation. How would I be viewed if I take up with a married woman? I know her husband deserted her nearly a year ago and is quite likely dead..."

"And how did you get there Conrad?"

"It's the truck. Julia told me that Brett would never let her drive his truck. So he is either living in some country where you can't drive a truck or dead."

"What about in prison?"

"Julia checked when he first went missing and she used to do a series of monthly phone calls to the police, the hospitals in the area, things like that. So it's not only my reputation, but her reputation that I am worried about as well. I like it here in Huckleberry. I don't want people thinking that I took advantage of a naive young woman and run me out of town."

Gracie clucked her tongue. "Conrad, you're a home owner now. Nobody can 'run you out of town' for bad behavior. What are the other issues troubling you?"

"Julia told me she stopped phoning; she stopped searching for her husband months ago. She told me there was no point. It

Gore in the *Garden*

worries me. In prison I learned to be highly sensitive to bull..." Conrad stopped what he was going to say and amended the word. "Highly sensitive to balderdash. I don't think Julia is lying to me about anything, but the certainty she has that her husband is dead, truck usage aside, has me concerned."

Gracie got up and made a pot of herbal tea. "It has me concerned as well. Anything else?"

"Oddly enough, my Mom had some beautiful clothing. When I was about twelve, she just started wearing pajama's all the time. I had completely forgotten about her dresses and pantsuits and things until I started cleaning out the house. She kept her clothes in garment bags, so they all look brand new. I would like to donate the whole works of them, but I really don't want to see anybody else wearing them. Does that make sense?"

Gracie got up and gave Conrad a hug. Zoey put out a paw as if to say, 'he's mine' and left it there until Gracie placed the mug of cinnamon and orange blossom tea on the side table beside Conrad and returned to her own chair.

"I think I know what you mean. When my husband died, I finally emotionally able to donate his clothing about six months later. I couldn't bear to see anyone in his clothes, so I drove to a city about four hours away and dropped them in the donation bin there. Another thing, Conrad, not to be indelicate, but no self-respecting woman would wear a pantsuit these days. I think a lot of your Mom's clothing might not be, shall we say, fashionable and therefore not wearable."

Conrad sipped his tea. "You know, I did see a lot of shoulder pads in the blazers. But still, I'll do what you did. Drive to a city far away and donate them. I do have more issues if you have time?"

His hostess nodded.

"It's this lack of routine that's making me feel weird; unsettled. I wake up expecting bells to ring, people to be talking, guards to be telling me what to do. I now have the freedom I longed for, but I am more anxious than when I was in prison." Conrad sipped more tea. "It's almost as though I need an authority figure to be accountable to."

"To paraphrase a famous author, your mind needs discipline in order to know freedom. Set yourself up a routine and stick to it," Gracie advised.

"I'll give it a try. So my last issue for now is about Julia again. I don't really feel comfortable being alone with her and I just can't get a handle on her character. When we talk on the phone, the conversation starts off strong; we're laughing and joking, but then she seems to switch gears and dismisses me. I don't know how to get to know her better."

Gracie smiled. "One word. Bowling."

"What? You're joking, aren't you?"

She shook her head. "No Conrad, bowling brings a person's true colors to the fore. You may find out that you are, in fact, not a good sport when you lose." She pointed to herself and mugged. "You may also find out that you are very competitive and tend to get a little cutthroat." She again pointed to herself and made a face. "But the wonderful thing about bowling is that you can observe other people's qualities, both good and bad, while you're having fun! I just happen to be on a bowling team, and a temporary vacancy will be opening up while my friends Dave and Pauline Shufeldt are on vacation. You and Julia could come and join our team."

"I don't believe I've ever bowled in my life, but it looks like fun. I also like being able to check out if Julia is a good sport or not and find out if I'm one! I'll text her! What time?"

Gracie pursed her lips. "There is one drawback though, the name of our team. Because it's primarily made up of cops, and because most of us were too tipsy to register a better name, my boyfriend named us "The Huckleberry Blue Balls."

Conrad burst into laughter. He could not stop laughing. He finally gasped out, "It would be an honor to be on a team called the Huckleberry Blue Balls!"

Zoey sneezed several times. These humans could be disgusting at times. She then lifted her leg to begin grooming, but Conrad gently pushed her off his lap. She walked stiffly to the sunny spot in the front window. Yes, these humans were just disgusting.

***

Westminster chimes sounded as Trudy-Faye repeatedly pressed the doorbell.

The householder opened the door and said, "Isn't that the most beautiful sound ever? I could just stand here and listen to it over and over."

Julia Smith then reached in front of Trudy-Faye and pressed the bell again. "Isn't it just lovely?"

"This is an official visit, Julia. I've come to your home today as the President of the Garden Club. We are very displeased with this, this flower display." Trudy-Faye pointed in the direction of the four metal bedposts stuck in the ground. In between each set of two, a vibrant bed of marigolds shone.

Julia reached her hand out and poked Trudy-Faye in the stomach.

"Did we get up on the wrong side of the bed this morning?" she asked.

Trudy-Faye could not believe what just happened. This snippet of a girl was giggling and not taking Trudy-Faye seriously.

"Come here!" the President ordered and walked toward the marigolds. Unfortunately, she didn't realize that the heap of marigolds was due to the mound of dirt that covered a layer of concrete. Trudy-Faye's foot did not sink in the soil as she thought it would but banged into the edge of the concrete. Trudy-Faye yelled "Ow!" and fell over.

Julia was amused. "Would you like me to get you a pillow so you can sleep on my garden bed?" she asked. She walked over to where Trudy-Faye was lying. With a sweep of her arm, Julia asked, "Or would you prefer to sleep on this bed?"

Trudy-Faye groaned and said, "You idiot!". She attempted to sit up but ended up rolling towards Julia.

Julia looked at the crushed flowers and frowned.

"Excuse me, Trudy-Faye Gervais, but I'd like you to know that I do read. As the owner of this property, and according to Huckleberry residential zoning laws, I have the right to augment, decorate or otherwise adorn my property so long as no injury befalls any persons or animals or impedes their right of way on a public sidewalk."

Trudy-Faye's jaw dropped.

"You are welcome to lay there until you feel ready to leave but don't linger. I'm sure the Garden Club needs their President for important matters."

Julia started to walk away and then snapped her fingers. She remembered something else she had read in a book once.

"I'd like you to think about what you've done and when you have formulated your apology, you may deliver it to me in person." Julia went to walk away again, but turned back and said, "And I'll give you a hint about the things you should apologize for: you have ruined my flowers, insulted me and my home and you are masquerading as some sort of authority on gardening when your own yard looks like a dog's breakfast." Julia said all this without rancor or raising her voice. She smiled, "Toodles."

Gore in the *Garden*

Trudy-Faye decided she would just lay there and re-group, but the oddest smell seemed to be coming from the marigolds. Like something had crawled in a hole and died. Probably the sewer line, she thought. She quickly got up, looked at Julia's front door and decided not to do two things. She would not tell Julia about the suspected break in the sewer line, and she certainly would not apologize.

Julia watched through the curtains as Trudy-Faye walked quickly to the street and got in her car. Julia had decided to not do a couple things as well. One, she would not insist on an apology and two, she would not tell Trudy-Faye that she had a marigold stuck to her behind.

***

"I'm just supposed to knock down those pins with this ball?" Julia asked.

"Basically yes. Just throw the ball and then we can see what you've got. Don't worry, we know you haven't bowled before," Gracie said good naturedly. She was pleased that Conrad had asked Julia to join them.

The Huckleberry Blue Balls had their shoes on and were ready to roll with their substitute team members, Julia Smith, and Conrad Jeffries. Julia wanted to go first.

Julia looked at the Gracie, Ted, Mark and Conrad and asked again, "Just knock down those pins with this ball? You guys aren't pulling my leg are you?" She turned, picked up the first ball with her right hand and without any pause, took three steps and smoked the ball down the lane. She hit just to the right of the one pin. She got a strike.

"That's all you do?" she asked, still worried the group was somehow pulling a prank.

The group had been stunned into silence. After Julia asked her question, they broke into loud cheering.

"Unbelievable!"

"Way to go!"

"Beginner's luck!"

"Do it again!"

Julia frowned. "You want me to throw another ball down? But I knocked everything down already."

"Turn around dear and look, the pins are automatically being set up again," Gracie advised.

Without a word, Julia picked up a ball and got another strike. When she was told to do it again, she did it again.

"This is the most annoying game. I knock the pins down and that machine just keeps setting them up. What's the point?"

Gracie and Conrad tried to explain the scoring and encouraged Julia to watch the fun the other players were having; but Julia wasn't convinced.

"Sorry folks, this game is really boring." She started to untie her shoes but stopped when she saw Conrad looking surprised and a little bit sad.

"I'll stay and watch you guys. It's nice getting out of the house and doing stuff with people."

About the sixth frame, Julia was amazed. Most of the folks on the team had difficulty throwing what they called strikes. Every time she was told to throw the ball and knock the pins down, she did.

She was well on her way to a perfect game and a buzz was building through the bowling alley. Even Trudy-Faye was excited.

Unfortunately, Julia thought it would be more fun to try and pick the pins off one at a time so for her next turn she threw the ball and knocked only the headpin down.

The entire Splitsville Lanes groaned in unison.

Julia explained what she was doing to the team. They in turn tried to explain the scoring again but stopped when they realized how much fun she was having.

"I'm going to get us some soft drinks," Conrad said.

"I'll join you," Gracie replied.

As they walked to the counter, Conrad lowered his voice and said to Gracie, "You were right about bowling. I'm fascinated by her; she's definitely a good sport even though she doesn't get the sport. But there's something not quite…" He stopped and tried to put his feelings into words. "There's nothing wrong with her; she's delightful, but, perhaps this is crass, you know the saying "one sandwich short of a picnic'?"

Gracie nodded and added, "But she's very intelligent. She's not missing a sandwich, it's just like she just didn't want one, so she didn't bring it."

"Something like that. I enjoy listening to her talk; I never know what she's going to come up with. But did you notice at the beginning when she was bored? I thought she was going to hop in her truck and drive away."

"Yes. Her sudden drop in energy was noticeable. She may just be a person who has to have something on the go all the time."

Conrad laughed. "You know Gracie, I think you might be able to identify with her."

As they picked up the pop and snacks, Gracie said wryly, "Have you seen my newspaper ad?"

***

At the Gervais home, Trudy-Faye was at her computer, reading the news from the Huckleberry Bulletin website. Evelyn Pitre's trial was still months away as she was claiming diminished capacity.

And she might have a point there. Anyone who brings their husband lunch and on the spur of the moment decides to stab them in the neck might have a few mental health issues. Her lawyer had already delayed the trial twice for psychological assessments.

"William, you know what this means?"

William knew Trudy-Faye would just talk herself into a decision; the only thing he needed to contribute to the conversation was the occasional grunt.

"The Pitre home won't be going up for sale for some time. They didn't have any kids you know; what a shame. That big old house just standing empty."

William Gervais Senior gave a non-committal grunt.

"So I think I'll hold off approaching the lawyer for the listing. That will give Julia Smith time to get her sewer fixed. She's not such a bad gal after all; she did alright at bowling tonight. What do you think William?"

William didn't know if he was supposed to comment on Julia Smith's bowling prowess, sewer fixing plans or Trudy-Faye's listing delay.

He grunted.

***

Under the marigold beds, Brett Smith's body continued to decompose. Normally, his wife would come out each night and talk to him. But, after bowling, Julia Smith did not go out to the marigolds to talk to Brett. She had spent months proving to Brett and herself that all the things he had said to her were untrue. She was talked out.

Plus, she liked talking to real people better.

Gore in the *Garden*

What Happens When The Cabbage Leaves?

Shirley Vallencourt was thinking of gophers. Years ago she had travelled to Yukon on her honeymoon with her new husband Landon. She had told him that she was a big fan of the poetry of Robert Service, so he surprised her with a flight north where a rental car was waiting in Whitehorse. They then drove further north to 'the marge of Lake Laberge' to read poetry and eat their lunch.

Like most newlyweds, they were broker than broke, so they ate cheese and crackers. Out of nowhere, an artic ground squirrel popped up on the rock beside them and began eating the crumbs. The squirrel was huge! Shirley and Landon began breaking pieces off the cracker and throwing it to him. Several more squirrels showed up.

"We're surrounded!" giggled Shirley.

The first squirrel was greedy; he pounced on every piece of cracker before his smaller cousins could even try. In fact, he was stuffing his mouth so fast and so full, that just as soon as he shoved cracker in one side of his mouth, crumbs were falling out of the other side. The smaller squirrels were busy licking up the crumbs.

Shelley Dawn Siddall

Landon and Shirley laughed and laughed.

That was then. Things pretty much went downhill in the years since their honeymoon.

Now, Landon was nothing but a greedy ground squirrel. Money was everything to him. He was so concerned about stuffing their bank accounts with money, that he spent five days a week living in the city and just coming home on the weekends. Their bank account was more than healthy; their marriage was not.

It's true that Shirley loved not having to work for a living, but the more money Landon made, the tighter he got with the household budget. Last weekend, he had slashed Shirley's household allowance.

It started after Shirley bought a plastic bottle of water at the gym for two dollars.

"You paid for water? Are you crazy? I'm away working in the city all week and you're at home wasting my hard-earned money?"

He stood there waiting for her to answer.

Shirley was flabbergasted but being married to Landon for the last fifteen years, she knew it was pointless to argue. This was not the hill she was going to die on.

"I'll remember to pack my water bottle next time I go," she wearily said.

"And what do you need to go to the gym for? What's the point? You look the same as when we got married."

Shirley felt her ire rise. "That is the point, Landon. I work hard at keeping my figure, so I go to the gym!"

Landon slammed his hand down on the kitchen counter.

"No more. You're done. You've got enough to do out in the yard and cooking and keeping this house clean. You don't need to go to the gym and associate with those idiots."

Gore in the *Garden*

Shirley was completely angry now. "I am not cancelling my membership! I love going to the gym. A lot of my friends go there; we go to the same classes."

Landon raised his hand and threatened to hit her.

It was enough. She backed down.

"I'll phone and cancel," she said.

Having won, Landon's temper switched off. "Whatever you're making for supper smells awesome. I'm glad I married such a good little cook." He gave her a wink and went to the den to watch the news.

It took some time for Shirley's breath to return to normal. She busied herself with making a salad with all her fresh garden vegetables.

She promised herself, 'One of these days, I'm going to fight back. I don't care if I get another black eye or even lose my teeth, I'm going to fight back'.

The couple continued on for another week, then Landon came home and found something else that Shirley needed to cut back on.

"No more of these annuals. You don't need to be continually buying seeds and starter plants for flowers and things that only last a couple of months. No. It's just a waste of money and it's stopping now."

"But our salads are all annual plants…" Shirley began.

"No buts!" Landon thundered. "No excuses just do it. I want you to stop growing annuals right now! Today! Or else!"

"Fine."

Shirley was starting to boil; but she kept a lid on her temper. As soon as Landon left for work that week, she got out the newspaper where she had an ad circled. It read:

Shelley Dawn Siddall

"Did you do something bad, but can't quite remember? Did your neighbor do something bad, and you want to get the goods on them? Contact Gracie Noseworthy Investigations at 555-2368. I sniff out trouble!"

"Is this Gracie Noseworthy?"

"Yes, what do you need investigated?"

"Could I meet you somewhere, maybe at the park? I don't want to talk about this at a coffee shop. Some of my husband's friends could be there."

Mrs. Shirley Vallencourt was a slim woman, only slightly shorter than Gracie, with beautiful salt and pepper hair. They met on the bench by the duck pond.

"I wish my hair was as gorgeous as yours!" Gracie said as they shook hands.

"I get black lowlights put in. My husband thinks it's all natural, but I sneak off to the beauty salon every so often and get it done."

Gracie's mental notetaking went like this, "Good quality clothing, but at least fifteen years old and in need of repair. Husband a miser? Purple and yellow bruising around the left eye; she's wearing a turtle neck with long sleeves in summer; abused?" What she said was, "Where do you get the money to pay the hairdresser?"

"I take the runners from my strawberry plants and pot them and sell them when my husband is away in the city working. My husband Landon is a bit of a tightwad." Shirley was sitting with her back straight as a board, and a bead of sweat was across her brow from both the turtleneck and her nervousness.

Gracie put her hand over Shirley's. "Just tell me," she said softly.

"I can't live at home any longer, but I'm too afraid to make any changes. As a joke, my husband and I signed pre-nuptial agreements. If I leave the marriage, I will get nothing. I've never worked in my life, Gracie, I don't know how I would support myself."

"Even in little old Huckleberry, there are a lot of organizations that can help you with that. But before we go there, what did your husband's prenup say?"

Shirley gave a quick smile. "He was so in love with me and thought I was in his words, the 'most perfect specimen of womanhood', so we wrote in his if he commits adultery all our joint money belongs to me."

Gracie admired the mallard ducks floating on the pond. These little creatures mate for life without prenuptials, bank accounts or flashy cars. Just enduring friendship governed by instincts. Maybe we should all be robots and have kindness pre-programmed into us? She asked Shirley, "What do you suspect?"

"I find random things in his pockets. As stereotypical as it sounds, receipts for lingerie, flowers, and wine. He always has a glib answer; it was a purchase he made on behalf of a client. Landon's in sales."

"You think he has a lover. Any other evidence?"

"He has always been a tightwad, but the past three months he has been laying down the law, as he calls it. His latest command is that I can't buy any more annuals. He says anything but perennials is a waste of money. I tried to tell him that the ingredients for all those salads and vegetables we both love to eat, are grown from our garden, but he wouldn't even listen. He just shut me down." Shirley sighed and although she was looking out at the pond, she didn't see anything.

"I have to say this Shirley. If you are being abused, you should leave the home immediately. At no time is physical or emotional abuse something you have to live with. And be warned, it will just escalate; each so called honeymoon period where Landon is all lovey-dovey will grow shorter and shorter until you are just living a life of terror, day in and day out."

The two women sat in silence. Finally Shirley spoke up, "I've looked up the resources before; I just can't take that step."

"I'd never force you to," Gracie said, "So, what would you like me to investigate?"

"Is my husband cheating on me in the city? If he is, can you find me a lawyer? Landon checks all my incoming and outgoing calls. That's why I was so short on the phone. I'm going to say it was a wrong number."

Gracie shook her head. "Oh don't do that. You heard from a friend that I have a lot of peony tubers that I give away for free. You phoned to see if I have any left and then came over to my house to pick them up."

"Good plan!"

The two women left the park, and each drove their vehicle to Gracie's home.

Gracie brought out a paper bag from her house.

"I've cut off the foliage and the roots and cleaned the tuber and then wrapped each one in newspaper. Just keep them in a cool dark place in your house, and next spring plant them and you'll have gorgeous pink peonies!"

"Thanks Gracie. What do I owe you for everything?"

Gracie put her hands on her hips. "We're going to take a long term view of this investigation. Besides my initial one hundred dollar fee, there will be some costs involved as I travel to the city and investigate. You will pay me, but I am entirely amenable to accepting one strawberry plant a year if there is no evidence of adultery. If there is adultery and a divorce, you can pay me when you get your settlement; although, I could use a strawberry plant in the meantime."

Gore in the *Garden*

The two women shook hands and parted ways. Each felt a heaviness in her heart that had not been there first thing in the morning.

***

Shirley just wanted everything done and over with, but she knew, like Gracie, it was going to be a long haul. Landon was intelligent; he would cover his tracks.

If he had tracks to cover. Maybe he was just buying that stuff for a client and the client would pay him back? Sure, he just happened to shop for wine late at night from room service at a fancy hotel.

Shirley could not understand how she could waffle like this; one moment absolutely convinced she was being cheated on and the next, defending her husband. Nor could she comprehend her refusal to call his abuse, abuse.

Without warning, all the excuses started running through her head; he was tired, he was stressed from work, her tone of voice was harsh, she shouldn't talk back, he had a right to tell her how to spend the money because he earned it.

And the worst one, he didn't mean it; he loved her. Well, we'll just see about that when he comes home next week and sees what I've done, Shirley thought.

She put the paper bag with the peony tubers in a drawer in her craft room. Shirley was going to order out for her supper when the beeping sound of the front door lock began. Landon walked in.

"Hi, what brings you back home?" she asked surprised that after one night in the city he returned home. Normally, he rented a room from a co-worker for the week.

"Can't a man come home when he wants to?" Landon snarled.

"I'm sorry, I was just wondering why you came home early. Is everything all right?"

"What makes you think I did something wrong? Women, always suspecting the worst. It's none of your business why I'm home. Just put supper on the table like you're supposed to."

Shirley decided then and there that she should be treated with dignity. Thus, it was nothing big that finally flipped the switch in Shirley. She was worthy and would stand up for herself.

"About supper," she said. "I've abided by the rules you gave me yesterday when you told me to stop growing annuals."

"Good! About time you listened to me," said Landon as he went to the fridge in search of a cold drink.

"What the hell?" he said, as he opened the fridge. Normally it was stuffed with vegetables cut bite size for snacking. There was nothing in the fridge but milk and frozen meat.

Shirley began speaking slowly and continued to talk even though Landon was getting angrier and angrier.

"You said to stop growing annuals. As I tried to explain yesterday, carrots are annuals, lettuce is an annual, radishes are annuals, cabbages are annuals, peas, pumpkins, beets, beans, tomatoes are all annuals. You get the idea. So, as per your wish. I stopped growing them all immediately. I got out the rototiller and plowed the vegetable gardens under."

It had been a bad day already for Landon. His firm's number one client fired the firm citing irreconcilable creative differences. It may also have been due to the fact that Landon had been sleeping with the client's wife who decided to return to her husband because Landon was not able to 'keep her in the style to which she was accustomed'. Landon's firm, in turn, fired him. And now, his wife was talking back to him? What in the world was going on?

Gore in the *Garden*

He raced to the kitchen door and looked out the window. Sure enough, just huge patches of dirt remained. Landon had never been so angry; he could barely see as his vision went black.

Landon clenched and unclenched his hands and ran towards Shirley. She was going to pay for this big time.

She stood her ground. In fact she took two steps towards him and pointed her finger at him.

"This is your anger, and I will not be a victim of it. I am dialing 911 right now. I am also walking out the front door. You will not lay a hand on me."

Shirley began talking to the operator on the phone indicating a domestic abuse situation and giving her address. The police car had been patrolling the area and was there almost as soon as Shirley walked out the door.

Landon attempted to charm the police officers.

"Look officers, the little lady got her knickers in a twist because I wanted my supper early. No problem, I'll wait. Just tell her to get back in here and make it and everything will be fine."

Shirley did not even look back. She told Constable Dave, "I'm going to need a ride to a woman's shelter. I will not stay here and be beaten up."

As Shirley sat in the back of the police car, she heard Landon shouting then screaming at the officers to force his wife to return.

She had done it. She had escaped, but there was no sense of relief. Time was standing still. She felt nothing.

***

Landon was allowed to stay in the marital home for now. He watched the police car drive off with his wife and then stormed back in the house and slammed the front door.

'She will pay, oh she will pay' was the mantra going through his mind. His wife had humiliated him, and he was going to get even. He ran to her craft room determined to destroy everything in it. He pulled down bookcases and grunted as he pushed over a filing cabinet. He opened the closet and threw all her carefully ordered sewing and knitting projects on the floor. He lifted up her sewing machine high over his head then dropped it.

He was going to tip over her desk when he noticed the drawer. He dumped the contents on the ground and a few of the peony tubers wrapped in newspaper rolled out of the bag.

Landon picked one up and unrolled it.

"Ah ha!" he yelled, "Holding out on me you sneak!" He sniffed the tuber. "What is this? Ginger? No, must be some kind of weird turnip."

He tried a little bite, but it was too bitter. He stomped toward the kitchen as he hollered, "Oh no lady, you are not going to get one over on me! I found your stash of food and I'm going to eat it."

Landon was pumped. In his rage fueled brain, he had overcome the defeats of the day with this tiny victory. He found a jar of relish, chopped up the tuber and ate it. With relish. He laughed heartily at his own joke. Just wait until Shirley came home and saw her craft room! She was going to go ballistic.

And Landon would stand there watching her cry. He rehearsed what he was going to say, "You take something from me? I take something from you. Have you learned your lesson woman? Get supper on the table and clean up this mess."

Landon went back into the craft room and ripped the quilted artwork off the walls and stomped on it. He then picked up all the remaining wrapped tubers and brought them back to the kitchen. He was going to eat them all. That would serve her right.

Gore in the *Garden*

As he ate another and another, he was finding it more and more difficult to choke them down. But he was determined. He finished the entire jar of relish and the peony tubers at the same time.

***

In Huckleberry that night, several interesting conversations were being held.

Barry Frederickson was reassuring Barbara Shire that she would make a fine mother; they would raise this child together. It didn't matter what kind of mother Barbara had; they would never abandon their child. And they could name them Bart or Brenda; wouldn't that be nice?

Anderson Payne had phoned Maureen Smiley to inform her that he had prepared an instruction manual on how to build a Koi Pond and he could mail it to her if she liked. Maureen let Anderson know that they were going to have macaroni and cheese and would be delighted if he would join her and Tracy. Mind you, she went on to say, he would have to tell Tracy all about his fish; did he think he could handle it?

Fred Downton was sitting in his living room talking to his computer through a dictation program Byron Eggplant had set up for him. Fred was saying all the things he had ever wanted to say to his mother. Byron was prompting him by saying things like, 'and you were how old at this time?' and 'could you explain a bit more about what was going on in your life at the time?'.

Byron was finally calm. Everything was coming together. After all he was helping his idol write and discover his process and life couldn't get better than this, could it?

Conrad Jeffries was writing poetry and reading out loud to himself.

Shelley Dawn Siddall

"If I nurture grief, does it blossom? Can you only grieve for someone lost? What about heartbeats imagined? I guess this is all part of the process, isn't it?"

Anita Ellis was trying to win over her pro bono lawyer. He didn't think she was a really bad person, did he? Did he know he had the cutest dimples when he smiled? If she knew where some large sums of money were, he wouldn't have to report that would he?

Gracie Noseworthy and Ted Bailey were having an animated conversation about their place in Munson. They would need a screened-in sun room for the kitties, wouldn't they? And how about one of those hot water on demand tanks; it doesn't make any sense to heat gallons of water year 'round for a weekend retreat, does it? And we should give some thought to the landscaping, because if we ever did get married, that would be the spot to do it, don't you think?

Trudy-Faye and William Gervais were going through an old baby album. He really is dead isn't he? I wonder if he had any children with that woman over in Munson? It's crazy to hope we could be grandparents, isn't it? Would she want to get to know us, do you think?

Julia Smith was at the pound talking to a beagle. You will be my little buddy, won't you? You and I will have great fun gardening won't we? What do you think of the name Bernard? Oh, you like it do you?

Hazel Froment and Shane Mitchell were watching television and eating supper together. You're not bored of my stories are you? What if you tell me some of yours? Oh my goodness, you are way more interesting than me, aren't you?

Gore in the *Garden*

Jasmine Summan was having her regular evening chat with a man she had known for weeks. No my dear, I can't do that, it's completely illegal, isn't it?

Myron and his Father were discussing a course of action. It's got to be done, doesn't it? It's just about time, isn't it?

Mrs. Shirley Vallencourt in the Women's Shelter, holding the threadbare towels she had been given and receiving instructions about meal times, cleaning times and general rules of the house. This was tough but better than being at home, wasn't it? She still couldn't see properly out of her left eye; she should go to a Doctor about that shouldn't she?

Landon Vallencourt wasn't talking to anyone. He had been in agonizing pain earlier but was too stubborn to phone for help. He died that night, poisoned by the gift of peony tubers given to his wife by Gracie Noseworthy.

So as it turned out, Gracie didn't have to go into the city to investigate after all.

***

If you enjoyed this novel, you might enjoy my 'Murder She Read Mystery' series. The first book is called **'Bury the Lead'** and is available on Amazon.

Shelley Dawn Siddall

About the Author

Shelley was thrilled with the original Kirk, Spock, and the gang when they were first introduced on television. Science Fiction was a powerful force in introducing squirrels (some say Tribbles) into her brain.

The squirrels have been chattering ever since and over the years have become voracious readers of many genres. That's why Shelley writes in so many different genres. She is also pioneering a grittier form of cozy mysteries, not too graphic but with a dash more of the thriller genre. All her novels are available on Amazon.

Between knitting and volunteering, she writes and tends her gardens. Whoa. That sounds fairly bucolic, doesn't it? And yet she writes about murders. Makes one wonder what's really under the sod...

Shelley has really enjoyed some of her varied careers-loans officer, autobody repair (that's right, she learned how to re-core a radiator) coffee pourer, tree chopper, and a nurse in long-term care. She loves listening to people talk about their lives. Shelley then lets all these experiences percolate, distill, and reduce into unique characters in her novels.

Gore in the *Garden*

Shelley has a tiny YouTube channel where she reads all the poems in this novel and some from the first book of 'Chickens in Sweaters and other epic poems'. She also reads a bit from one of her romantic comedies.

She lives in a little trailer near a lake and finds inspiration in the compassion of others.

Thank you again for reading my novel.

Made in United States
Troutdale, OR
07/14/2023